Juanita Fights
the School Board

Books in

THE ROOSEVELT HIGH SCHOOL SERIES

Juanita Fights the School Board

by
GLORIA VELÁSQUEZ

PIÑATA BOOKS
ARTE PÚBLICO PRESS
HOUSTON, TEXAS

This book is made possible through a grant from the National Endowment for the Arts (a federal agency), the Lila Wallace-Reader's Digest Fund and the Andrew W. Mellon Foundation.

Piñata Books
An Imprint of Arte Público Press
University of Houston
452 Cullen Performance Hall
Houston, Texas 77204-2004

Piñata Books are full of surprises!

Cover illustration and design by Vega Design Group

♾ The paper used in this publication meets the requirements of the American National Standard for Permanence of Paper for Printed Library Materials Z39.48-1984.

9 0 1 2 3 4 5 6 7 8   13 12 11 10 9 8 7 6

For my children,
Brandi, Bobby and Angelito

ONE
Juanita

It's the worst Friday of my life. Not only do I get up late, but by the time I finally get out the door, Rina and the guys have already left without me. I end up walking to school all by myself. I hate walking alone. Then when I get to my locker, Maya has already gone to her first period class. I grab my books and race to my English class, stepping inside the room just as the tardy bell rings. I can feel everyone staring at me. I hate that.

I sit down as quietly as possible, wondering what in the heck the teacher is diagramming on the board. My head jerks up when I hear my name called over the intercom, telling me to report to the Dean of Students. I get up again, feeling so nervous that I almost trip over the seat in front of me. Someone laughs, but I ignore it.

In the main office, Mr. Jones is waiting for me. I follow him into his office and he asks me to sit down. He begins by telling me how sorry he is about everything that has happened. I can barely keep the tears from coming when he tells me that I have been expelled from school for the entire year. He tells me again how sorry he is and that the principal has agreed to let me finish out the first

7

quarter since there is only one week left.

I don't cry in front of him. I just nod my head and let him do all the talking. Afterwards, I race to the girls' bathroom. I flush the toilet so that no one will hear me cry. When the bell rings, I wash my face quickly and walk back to my locker, blinking back the tears. What will I tell my 'Amá and 'Apá? Now I probably won't graduate. And 'Apá is so proud of me, always bragging to his friends that I will be his first daughter to graduate from high school. Now what will he say to them?

I jerk open my locker door and grab my books for my next class.

"Hey, Johnny. What's bugging you? Are you on the rag?"

It's Maya, my best friend. I always tell her everything. I turn around to look at her.

"They just kicked me out of school, out of the whole district. I can't come back at all," I blurt out. Maya lets her backpack fall to the floor.

"What? Are you crazy? They can't do that to you just because of the fight. Who told you that nonsense, the principal?"

I can't help but smile at Maya. She thinks everyone is a fool.

"That's what Mr. Jones just finished telling me. 'Apá will kill me when he finds out," I answer. I feel the tears coming again and the next thing I know, Maya has her arm around me.

"Don't worry, Johnny. They can't kick you out just like that."

"I'm so scared, Maya. What am I going to do now?" I ask.

"I'm not sure," Maya says, getting quiet. Then all of a sudden she gets an excited look on her face.

"Wait a second. I think I know someone who might be able to help. She's a friend of my mom's. Her name is Ms. Martínez. She's some kind of shrink who helps our people all the time. I'll tell my mom to call her tonight. Maybe she can help you. She's always helping my mom's friends. Don't worry, Johnny. Here, wipe your face," Maya says, handing me a Kleenex.

"Thanks, Maya," I answer, blowing my nose. "I am already starting to feel a little bit better."

"Come on, the bell's about to ring. We'll be late for History."

I close my locker and follow Maya down the hallway.

Later, while Mr. Kiley is lecturing about the Civil War, I think about what Maya said. Maya is right. They can't do this to me. It isn't fair. Maybe Maya's mother can help me. I don't know what I'd do without Maya. She always knows what to do. She's so smart, not dumb like me. And her parents are smart, too. I wish my 'Amá and 'Apá were more like them. I have to talk to them in Spanish all the time. Sometimes it's embarrassing 'cause everyone stares at us. That's why I have to stay in school, learn English real good. I wonder what my 'Apá will do when he finds out I've been kicked out of school.

✎   ✏   ✐

At home that evening, I can't seem to concentrate on anything. At the supper table, I'm very quiet. I avoid looking into 'Amá's eyes. She gets a worried look on her face and asks me if I'm getting my period. I tell her no, that I'm just tired from

P.E. How will I explain everything to her and 'Apá? To my brothers and sisters? Carlos hasn't come home yet from football practice. I wonder if he knows already. I'm so nervous that my stomach hurts.

After Celia and I wash the dishes, we take the three little ones outside to the playground. I hardly talk at all, so Celia keeps bugging me, asking me if I'm in love. She's only thirteen. Boy crazy. I tell her to shut up, and I go back inside. I tell my 'Amá I have a headache and go upstairs to my room.

'Apá is not home yet. He works in the fields with some of his friends. Sometimes Carlos and I help him on weekends, but I hate it. My back always hurts, and it's burning hot. I'd rather stay home and watch the three little ones. I don't want to work in the fields when I'm big. But now I don't know. Maybe I'll never graduate. Maybe I'll have to work in the fields like 'Apá. Maybe Maya is wrong. Maybe I'm just another dumb Mexican, like the white kids call us. I turn my radio on, and I cry myself to sleep.

TWO
Juanita

The next morning, I feel someone pulling at my hair. It's my baby brother Markey. He's the youngest of the three little ones. I ask him what he wants and he tells me, *pipí*. I call him a brat and get out of bed quickly so that I can take him to the bathroom before he wets his pants. He's only three so he still has accidents.

When Markey is finished using the bathroom, I chase him back downstairs. I start to get dressed, remembering that it's Saturday and I don't have to hurry. I can smell 'Amá's tortillas, and suddenly I feel hungry. Celia is still sleeping. The phone rings and 'Amá hollers at me in Spanish that it is Maya. I hurry downstairs to the telephone. The three little ones are sitting down watching cartoons.

"Hi, Maya."

"Hi, Johnny. Listen, my mom is going downtown, and she said she would drop me off at your house, if it's okay with you. And I've got good news. Last night she called Mrs. Martínez, I mean Ms. Martínez, that's what she likes to be called. Well, my mom told her about what happened to you, and Ms. Martínez was real nice. She said she would call you. We gave her your phone number."

11

My stomach is starting to hurt again. "*Híjole*, so soon? Well, I guess that's good, but I haven't told my 'Amá and 'Apá yet. A letter came for them, but they don't read English."

"Well, don't worry. Ms. Martínez is gonna help. Anyway, I'll be by around noon, okay?"

"Okay. I'll see you then. Bye." I hang up the phone, feeling a sense of relief. Maya and her mom sure work fast. I hear my mother calling me to come and eat, so I go into the kitchen and make myself a taco. I ask where Carlos is, and she tells me that he has gone to work with my 'Apá. Good, I think to myself. Now Maya and I can talk without him hearing us. Carlos can be such a pain. Just because he's the oldest, he thinks he can boss me around. And he loves to show off in front of Maya.

When I finish my taco, 'Amá reminds me that it's time to do the housework. I can see Celia coming down the stairs, and I holler at her to hurry and eat so that she can help me clean. She gives me a dirty look.

It's difficult being the oldest daughter. 'Amá expects so much from me. But Maya says I'm lucky. She doesn't have any brothers and sisters; it's just her and her mom and dad. She can't understand what a pain brothers and sisters can be—always following you around, always needing help with something. Sometimes I just wish they'd all disappear, especially Celia. She never wants to do her share of the housework. 'Amá always has to yell at her.

By noon I have vacuumed, dusted, and given Markey a bath. Celia is angry at me because she got stuck with the kitchen and the bathrooms. That's what she gets for getting up so late. When she gives me a dirty look again, I remind her that we take turns, and that last week I did the toilets.

I decide to take a shower since Maya is not here yet. I turn the water on as hot as I can stand it. I'm beginning to feel nervous again, and a hot shower always relaxes me. What will 'Apá do when I tell him about getting kicked out? How embarrassing! I never imagined this would happen to me. I sure hope Ms. Martínez can help. Maybe she can explain it to my 'Apá, and then he won't be so mad. I step out of the shower and get dressed in a pair of shorts and an old T-shirt. I start to blow-dry my wavy hair. I hate my hair so much. I wish it were long and straight like Maya's. I'm putting on some makeup when Celia knocks on the door.

"Maya is here. Hurry up!" she yells at me.

As I start downstairs, I can hear Maya's voice. She loves to practice her Spanish with 'Amá. I smile as I listen to 'Amá invite Maya to sit down and eat. 'Amá thinks Maya is too skinny. She wants to fatten her up, but it doesn't seem to bother Maya. She always tells me how much she loves 'Amá's cooking.

✎   ✐   ✎

When Maya finishes eating the taco 'Amá made her, we go upstairs to my room. I have to bribe Celia with my new lipstick so that she will leave us alone. Celia's too nosy, always wanting to spy on us. She's worse than Carlos. Maya kicks off her sandals and we sit on the bed.

"Your mom makes the best tortillas. You know that?" Maya tells me.

Before I have time to answer, Maya says, "Ms.

Martínez is going to call you tonight. Okay?"

"*¡Híjole!*" I answer.

"Don't sweat it, Johnny. She's cool. You'll like her. Doesn't get on your nerves like my mom. Have you told your mom and dad yet?"

"Not yet. 'Apá left real early for work this morning."

"Well, Ms. Martínez said she would tell them if you wanted her to."

"'Apá is going to kill me. He thinks I'm doing good in school."

"Well, relax. Ms. Martínez said she would help, and she will. But you should try talking to your mom first. Didn't you say she always sticks up for you?"

"Yeah, that's true," I answer, knowing that Maya is right. I can always count on 'Amá's help. She always sticks up for me and Celia when 'Apá is mad. I remember the first time I wore makeup, how mad 'Apá got, telling me to go to the bathroom and wash my face; that no daughter of his would go around like a slut. But 'Amá had talked with him until she convinced him that it was all right to wear a little makeup. So 'Apá had agreed to let me wear a little eye-shadow and lipstick.

'Amá says 'Apá is old-fashioned and that that's the way the people from Mexico are. I'm sure glad I wasn't born there. 'Amá always tells me and Celia how strict her father was, never letting her go by herself anywhere, not even to the store. She talks about how she had to sneak out the window to go meet my 'Apá. Maya has it all wrong. She's the lucky one. Her mom and dad aren't so strict. They let her go everywhere she wants by herself.

"Come on, let's do our nails," Maya says, interrupting my thoughts.

We spend the next hour doing each other's nails and trying on my new makeup. Then Celia comes into the room to tell me that I have to take the three little ones to the playground while she and 'Amá go to the store.

Downstairs, Maya picks up Markey while I get my two little sisters, Lupita and Rosario, by the hand. We walk across the street to the small playground that faces the apartment complex. I hate going to the playground, but Maya doesn't seem to mind. She says it's fun watching all the people go in and out of their apartments, especially the cute guys.

I guess you can say we live in the barrio, as Maya calls it. It's the poorest neighborhood in the whole town—mostly blacks, Mexicans, and a few white people live here 'cause the rent is the cheapest. I used to get embarrassed when I told people where I live, but now I'm used to it. I can't understand why Maya likes it here. She lives in such a big pretty house, a whole bedroom to herself. Mostly rich people live where she lives. Maya says she hates it, that it's a boring place. I think she's crazy.

Maya pokes me on the side. "Look, there's Tyrone. I think he's so cute."

"He's staring at us. I think he likes you, Maya," I tell her.

"My mom and dad said they might let me start dating real soon. Maybe Tyrone will ask me out."

"Flirt!" I answer.

After about half an hour, Markey says he has to go *pipí*, so we go back to the apartment. I take him upstairs to the bathroom while Maya turns on the T.V. When I come back downstairs, Markey is sleepy, so I lay him on the couch. I chase my sisters into the other room. We are laughing and giggling about the weird bras the dancers are wearing on the music video when we hear a car honking. It's Maya's mother.

"Guess it's time to go," Maya says getting up from the couch. "Don't forget, Ms. Martínez is calling you tonight." As she opens the door, she adds, "Call me later. Bye."

      ✎   ✏   ✐

That evening, I'm sitting in the living room watching *Sábado Gigante* with 'Amá and 'Apá. They always watch this show on Saturday nights. I can't stand *Sábado Gigante*. Don Francisco is so stupid. They do the dumbest things on that show. The three little ones love to watch it. They think it's funny. The phone rings, and I race to get it. It's Ms. Martínez. She tells me that she is coming over tomorrow at two o'clock to talk to my parents. I try to tell her that my father always goes to his *compadre's* house on Sundays, but she says it's all right. When I hang up, my stomach is in knots. Celia asks me who it was and I lie. I tell her it was Maya. In the morning when 'Apá has left, I'll tell 'Amá about Ms. Martínez.

THREE
Juanita

The next day I feel so nervous that I pick on Celia for any little thing. I wait until 'Apá has left, and then I go downstairs to talk to 'Amá while she's cooking. I tell her about Ms. Martínez, that she is a counselor who wants to talk to us about school. 'Amá asks me if this has something to do with the fight. I nod my head, and she gets that worried look on her face that she always gets when 'Apá is drunk. I'm glad that she doesn't say anything else.

The day seems to go by slowly, even though I try to keep busy by doing the housework. Two o'clock finally arrives. My stomach is tied in knots so I decide to go outside and play catch with Markey. Every time a car drives by, my stomach tightens up even more. I am chasing Markey's ball across the street when I see a white Volkswagen pull up in front of the neighbor's apartment. Out of the corner of my eye, I watch as a pretty lady with short black hair gets out of her car and walks over to knock on the neighbor's door. She spots me as I walk back to where Markey is standing.

"Hello. I'm looking for the Chávez home. Do you know if I'm in the right place?" she asks me in a friendly voice. Markey starts to fuss. He is always shy around strangers so I pick him up.

"Hi. I'm Juanita Chávez. We live in this apartment," I answer.

Her face breaks into a big smile, and I can't help but notice her perfect white teeth. "Oh, how nice! I'm Ms. Martínez. Maya has told me all about you. Is that your little brother? He's so handsome."

"Yeah, his name is Markey. Come on in. My mom is inside," I tell her, opening the screen door. We go inside and I introduce her to my two little sisters, who are playing in the living room. She bends down to shake their hands and I notice she is wearing black stretch pants. I know 'Amá will think she's too skinny, like Maya. I go out to the back where 'Amá is hanging clothes and I tell her Ms. Martínez is here. 'Amá follows me back inside to the living room where Ms. Martínez is sitting down talking to Markey.

"Ms. Martínez, this is my mom. She doesn't speak English though," I tell her, wondering how she will react. Ms. Martínez stands up, and in perfect Spanish introduces herself to my 'Amá telling her that she is a counselor. I notice that her Spanish is better than Maya's and I can tell that 'Amá is impressed by this.

Before we all sit down, 'Amá yells for Celia to come downstairs. I introduce Celia to Ms. Martínez. I can tell that Celia is wondering what is going on, but she doesn't ask any questions. 'Amá asks her to take the three little ones out to the playground.

Ms. Martínez is the first to speak, praising my 'Amá for having such a nice family. 'Amá tells her that Carlos is the oldest, but that he isn't here. I can tell that 'Amá likes Ms. Martínez and I start to feel better.

In a soft voice, Ms. Martínez tells my mother about the school board's decision not to let me return to the school district. Before my 'Amá can say anything, Ms. Martínez tells her that she feels this is not a fair decision and that she wants to try and help me.

'Amá nods her head, telling Ms. Martínez that I am a good *hija* and that they have always tried to teach us how important school is. I'm embarrassed and I can feel my cheeks burning. Then Ms. Martínez tells my 'Amá that she knows I am a good girl and that she'll do everything she can to help me, but that I'll need to go visit her in her office next week. 'Amá says that she'll have to talk to 'Apá about it, but that she thinks he won't mind. Then 'Amá orders me to get Ms. Martínez a cup of coffee. I'm glad for an excuse to leave the room.

When I go back into the living room, Ms. Martínez and 'Amá are talking about Mexico. Ms. Martínez tells my 'Amá that her grandparents were from Juárez. I can tell that this pleases my 'Amá even more. Maya was right, she's very nice. I think I'm going to like her.

Before she leaves, Ms. Martínez gives me a big hug. Then she hands me a card with her name and address on it. I promise to go see her next week. I walk her to the door and watch as she crosses the street and gets into her little car. As she drives off, she honks the horn and waves.

Later that evening, I'm lying in bed trying to fall asleep when I hear loud voices. Celia whispers to me in the dark, "I think 'Amá and 'Apá are fighting." I tell her to be quiet and go to sleep. The next thing I know, Carlos is at the door, telling me that 'Apá wants to talk to me. I hurry downstairs. 'Apá is standing at the foot of the stairs. Before I can say anything 'Apá slaps me and tells me that it is wrong to fight, that he's ashamed of me. I can smell beer on his breath. 'Amá pulls him away and I run back upstairs, feeling my eyes fill with tears.

Carlos is standing in the hall, and he whispers to me, "I'm sorry. Are you all right?" I can barely answer him. I get back in bed, feeling scared and angry. Sometimes I hate 'Apá. Sometimes I hate my whole life.

FOUR
Juanita

By Tuesday, I'm sure that everyone at Roosevelt High knows that I've been kicked out and that this is my last week of school. No one dares to say anything, but I can tell by the looks of pity on their faces every time they see me. I avoid Sheena as much as possible. When she passes me in the hall, I look the other way. In my classes, I try to act as if nothing has changed. I pretend that everything is fine.

At noon, I sit with Maya and the rest of the gang in our usual spot out by the bleachers. They all try to cheer me up. Tommy even offers to help me with my math tonight. He knows how much I hate math. And Ankiza invites me to go downtown window shopping with her after school. Rina tells them both to shut up, that I haven't died yet. Maya laughs at them and turns the radio on to the rap station we all like. I can't imagine not being here at school with my friends, with Maya.

I think back to my freshman year at Roosevelt. There were only a few of us Mexicans, blacks, and Puerto Ricans, so we all just started hanging out together at lunchtime, forming our own group just like the socies and the heavy-metal kids. And at

school, everyone would stare at us. I remember
Rina's words, "Well, what do you expect from a
gringo town?"

And when Maya first came to Roosevelt, we all
thought she was stuck-up. She was on the tennis
team, and we all thought she was just another
air-head socie, so we gave her the cold treatment. I
remember that she would try to talk to us at
lunchtime, but we all ignored her. But then during
second semester, Maya and I were both in the same
Spanish class. That was when I found out that she
was a Mexican like me, and that she could speak
Spanish. The Spanish teacher, Mrs. Plumb, was
such a fool. Maya and I were the only ones who
could tell her Spanish was terrible since the rest of
the class was filled with *gabachos*. So we would giggle together, and when Mrs. Plumb would ask us a
question in Spanish, we would answer with words
she didn't really understand. This drove Mrs.
Plumb crazy.

By the end of that semester, Maya was eating
lunch with us. We all realized that she didn't want
to hang out with the socies, even though she was so
smart and pretty. Maya told us how she used to go
to school in the San-Francisco-Bay area and that
her best friends were Chicanos and blacks. She told
us about how her mom had been part of the Civil
Rights Movement and the Chicano Movement.

Maya calls herself a Chicana. She says I'm one
too 'cause I was born here in the U.S. I tell her I'm
Mexican, but she just laughs and calls me a *tonta*.

✎ ✏ ✐

After school, I usually walk home with Tommy,

Rina and Tyrone. We all live in the same neighborhood. Ankiza lives across town, where Maya does.
Maya thinks Tyrone is cute and she wishes she
didn't have to take the bus home. Maya says the
boys never notice her 'cause she doesn't have any
boobs.

Carlos has football practice every day, so he
never walks home with us. I'm glad 'cause he's too
bossy. He never wants me to look at any guys and
always tells me my skirt is too short. The only guy
he lets me talk to is Tommy. He says he thinks
Tommy is queer, but I tell him to shut up. I like
Tommy a lot. He's the only guy that Maya and I
can trust. He never rats on us or tries to hit on us.

Maya once asked me why we lived in a *gringo*
town, and I explained to her that here there are a
lot of farms and there's always work for 'Apá. I told
her how we used to live in Los Angeles, but my
'Apá couldn't find steady work so we moved out
toward Santa Barbara. From there, we just followed the work to this town. 'Amá says that if she
and 'Apá had stayed in Mexico, they would have
starved, and that's why they crossed the border. No
jobs there, living in shacks without electricity or
water. At least here, 'Amá says, we have a good
home. Maya says her grandfather on her mother's
side was from Mexico and also came over to work
in the fields like my 'Apá.

'Amá always has food waiting for us after
school. 'Apá doesn't get home until six or seven. It's
strawberry season and they work late. Celia is the
last one home from junior high. She comes on the
bus. Rosario and Lupita are in first and second
grade, so they get home a little bit before I do. They
are watching cartoons when I get home. Markey is

always excited to see me. He's so spoiled. After I eat, I go upstairs to my room. I can't decide if I should do my homework or not. It's my last week. Why bother? I remember Ms. Martínez then and my appointment with her on Friday. I decide to do my homework.

FIVE
Ms. Martínez

I glanced at my calendar. My appointment
with Juanita was not for another half hour. Good, I
had time to collect my thoughts. Frank's words
from this morning flashed before me: "Don't get so
over-involved, Sandy. You're always trying to save
the world. Haven't you learned by now that you
can't save everyone?"

Maybe Frank was right. I wasn't sure. All I
knew was that I was sick and tired of hearing
about all those minority kids who didn't make it
through high school. What good was my Ph.D. if I
couldn't help save one kid? No. Frank was wrong;
he was just acting like a concerned husband.
Someone had to help Juanita.

I leaned back in my chair and kicked off my
shoes, thinking back to my morning visit at
Roosevelt High School with the Dean of Students.
Mr. Jones, a tall, balding, fifty-year old man, had
appeared startled when I introduced myself politely as Dr. Sandra Martínez, telling him that I was
there on behalf of Juanita Chávez. When I asked
him about the expulsion hearing, it was very obvi-
ous that he wasn't accustomed to being questioned
by a woman, let alone a woman of color.

Mr. Jones began by indicating how distressed he was over the whole incident, adding very matter-of-factly, "The school administration feels very badly about the outcome, but Juanita has clearly violated school codes by committing battery on a student." Before I could respond, Mr. Jones extended an invitation for me to attend the expulsion hearing that had been scheduled in two days. He emphasized that it would be informal, composed of board members and some school administrators.

When I was finally allowed to speak, I answered as politely as I could, "Yes. I plan on being there so that I can assure that Juanita Chávez and her family are being treated fairly." I noticed a slight pink flush appearing on his face. But I needed to get things out in the open. "I am well aware that Roosevelt High School has a reputation for not being sensitive toward its few minority students," I added.

I knew what was coming. I had been through this so many times in the past. I watched as Mr. Jones leaned forward in his chair and, in a condescending tone, responded, "I beg your pardon. I am not aware of such problems. Roosevelt High prides itself in treating its students well. As Dean of Students, I personally ensure that all students are treated fairly here at Roosevelt High." Mr. Jones then proceeded to give me a five-minute biography of his experiences as a native of San Diego, working with minority students.

After a brief pause, I asked him point-blank, "Do you have any minority teachers on your staff?" I watched him closely as he attempted to straighten out his wide polka-dot tie. "Well, Mr.

Arias is from Spain. He teaches Spanish, and we
have one other teacher who is Portuguese. But, no,
at the moment, we don't have any blacks or
Mexican-Americans on our staff. The problem, you
see, is that there aren't enough of them out there
qualified like yourself," he said, winking at me.

"Oh, really, is that the problem?" I asked,
returning his sarcastic smile. I stood up to leave
and handed him my business card. Then I informed
him that I would be counseling Juanita on a regu-
lar basis. Mr. Jones shook my hand and said, "It's
been a pleasure. Perhaps we'll need your services
in the near future." I walked out of his office feeling
sorry for Juanita and all the other kids like her
who had to deal with a jerk like Mr. Jones on a
daily basis. It wasn't easy. I knew that only too well
because I had survived the same type of attitude
during my own high school years.

I sat up and looked at my calendar again. Two
days until the school board meeting. I felt my stomach muscles tighten. What would I say to them?
Maybe Frank was right. Maybe it was hopeless. No.
I couldn't allow myself to think like that. I needed
to think clearly. Be cautious. Advice, that's what I
needed. A woman's face flashed before me. What
was her name? I had met her at a panel discussion
on Latinas at the local university. Sharon Vargas.
Yes, that was it. Assistant District Attorney, a
high-powered Chicana who knew the legal system
well.

I reached for the phone book. Maybe this
woman could be of some assistance. It was worth a
try. I dialed the local District Attorney's office and
waited.

"District Attorney's office," announced a businesslike voice.

"Hello. I'd like to speak with Sharon Vargas."

"Her extension is 298. I'll ring for you."

A few seconds later, another voice answered, "Hello. Sharon Vargas here."

"Hello, Sharon. You probably won't remember me, but we met last spring. We were both on a panel discussing issues related to Latinas. I was discussing mental-health issues. My name is Sandra Martínez."

"Oh, of course. A great panel. A very good audience," she said.

"I remembered that you were an attorney and well, I was wondering if you might be able to help me." I spent the next ten minutes filling her in on what little information I had compiled about Juanita Chávez. Then I told her about my meeting with the Dean of Students and the upcoming board meeting.

Sharon listened patiently and then proceeded to warn me, "Let me give you some advice, Sandra. Don't go alone to that board meeting. Take an attorney with you. Those people are cutthroat. I was once involved with a similar issue and, from my experience with school boards, I would say the Chávez family needs legal representation."

"Do you really think so?" I asked. "They said it would be informal. Won't showing up with a lawyer antagonize the school administration further?"

"I repeat. Don't go without legal counsel. I wish I could help you, but since I work for the city government, I can't get involved in this."

"Well, the Chávez family doesn't have any money. The father is a migrant worker, doesn't even speak English. The mother stays home with the kids. I don't know how they could possibly afford an attorney," I answered, feeling nervous again.

There was a brief pause before Sharon spoke, "Let me see. I think I know someone who can help you. He's a friend of mine who sometimes takes clients with little or no money. His name is Sam Turner. He was involved with many Civil Rights cases in the '60s. A good man. Let me call him for you. Give me your home number and I'll get back to you tonight."

I gave Sharon my number, thanking her for all her help.

"No problem," she replied. "That's what we're here for, to help our community."

I hung up the receiver, feeling a sense of relief. Maybe things would turn out better than what I anticipated.

✎ ✏ ✐

Ten minutes later, I heard the bell at the reception desk ring. I slipped my shoes back on and hurried out to the front office to greet Juanita and her mother. My office, and those of two other therapists, was located in an old Victorian house that we rented on a monthly basis. We didn't have a receptionist, but handled our own appointments. The fact that this wasn't a formal office building made the environment more relaxed. Yet I knew how frightening and intimidating the first encounter was for the clients, especially for people of minority backgrounds.

I walked over to Juanita, who was standing next to her mother.

"Hello, Juanita," I said, noticing the worried look on Mrs. Chávez's face. "*¿Cómo está, Señora Chávez?*" I asked her in Spanish with the warmest smile I had. Mrs. Chávez's face seemed to relax as she politely answered. I turned to Juanita and asked her, "Should I call you Juanita or Johnny? Which do you prefer?"

"Everyone at school calls me Johnny, but you can call me Juanita if you want," Juanita answered.

"I like the sound of Spanish better, so I'll call you Juanita," I said. Then I switched back to Spanish and explained to Mrs. Chávez that she didn't have to stay for the appointment, only if Juanita wanted her to be present. I waited for Juanita to decide.

"Alone, if it's okay. My mom has my brothers and sisters waiting in the car."

I thanked Mrs. Chávez for coming and told her that I would give Juanita a ride home after our appointment. She thanked me and left. "Follow me, Juanita," I said, turning around the way I had come. "My office is in the back room."

Inside my office, Juanita was the first to speak. "Mrs. Martínez, I mean Ms. Martínez, my mom wanted me to ask you right away how much we would need to pay you."

"Don't worry about that now, Juanita. We'll work it out later. If you can give me one dollar each time we meet, that will be enough. But we can take care of that later. Now, please sit down."

Juanita sat down on the couch, nervously pulling at her skirt. I could tell that she was feeling very uncomfortable. "Juanita, I thought that for today maybe we could just spend time getting to know each other. Is that all right with you?" I asked.

"Yeah, I guess. I've never been to see a counselor before. Maya says you're a shrink and that only white people go see shrinks."

I couldn't help but laugh out loud. Juanita smiled, and I noticed that she was starting to relax. "That Maya is quite a character, isn't she?" I said.

"Yeah, I guess. She's my best friend at school."

I waited for Juanita to say something else, but she didn't. There was a moment of silence. Juanita was tugging at her skirt again. "I've got an idea. Why don't we talk about me first? I know you don't know anything about me except that I'm a shrink, as Maya put it, and that I'm a friend of Maya's family. You can ask me whatever you want. Okay?" Juanita's dark eyes were focused on me. There was a look of interest on her face.

"Okay," she answered. "How old are you?

"I'm really very old, thirty-six," I answered, smiling. Juanita smiled back at me and I noticed that she was really very pretty underneath all the eye-shadow.

"Are you married?" Juanita asked me.

"Yes, I am. Didn't Maya tell you that I'm married to a handsome *gabacho*?" Juanita was smiling again. Good. I wanted her to feel comfortable with me. "His name is Frank. He works as an accountant downtown. Any other questions?"

"Well, where did you learn to speak Spanish so good? My 'Amá really liked it that you spoke to her in Spanish."

"Good. Well, let's see. My grandparents on my mother's side were both from Mexico. My father came to the United States to work in the fields when he was young. My brother and I were both

born here and our parents taught us to speak
Spanish from the time we were babies. So I grew
up speaking two languages just like you. Any more
questions?"

Juanita was silent. I glanced at my watch.
Maybe it was time to switch gears. "Now, it's my
turn to ask questions. Are you ready?" I asked.
"You already told me that Maya is your best friend.
What's your favorite subject at Roosevelt?"

Juanita's face lit up and she answered without
hesitating, "I really love Spanish. Someday I want
to be a Spanish teacher."

"And I bet you'll be a very good one," I said.
"How do you like Roosevelt High?"

This time Juanita hesitated a little before
answering. "Well, I kinda like it, but it's kinda hard
going to a school with all whites and no Mexicans,
you know what I mean?"

Good. I was beginning to get somewhere, but I
had to proceed cautiously. "I know it can be difficult," I answered in a motherly tone

"But I like Roosevelt a lot," Juanita quickly
added. "It's just, well..." There was another
moment of silence before she completed her
sentence. "I just don't know what will happen now."
I watched carefully as a sad look invaded Juanita's
almond-shaped eyes. "I didn't mean to hit Sheena
so hard. I just wanted to put a stop to all her lies
about me and my family." Juanita's eyes were
watery now. "She was mad because my brother
Carlos didn't like her, so she was going around
saying bad things about us—that we were
wetbacks, things like that."

My mind suddenly flashed back to my own
high school years. Spics, greasers, beaners. I felt my

own eyes begin to blur and I bit my front lip. I had to get hold of myself if I was going to help her. Before I could react to Juanita's remarks, she burst into tears. I got up quickly and went to her side, putting my arm around her shoulder, "It's all right to cry, Juanita. Go ahead. I'll be right here to help you." I waited patiently as she cried. After a few minutes, I handed her a Kleenex. Juanita wiped her eyes and whispered, "I'm sorry, Ms. Martínez. I don't mean to act like such a baby."

"There's nothing to be sorry about. Why don't we stop for today? It's almost five o'clock. There's an ice cream parlor right around the corner from here. Doesn't that sound good?"

I saw a faint smile return to Juanita's face. "Okay, Ms. Martínez," she answered.

"Good girl. We'll grab our ice cream, then I'll drop you off, but you have to promise not to tell Frank. He thinks I'm on a diet."

Juanita grinned and said, "My 'Amá thinks you're too skinny."

"So does my mom," I told Juanita. This time we both laughed.

✎   ✐   ✎

Later that evening, the phone rang. "Hello," I answered, hoping that it was the call I was expecting.

"Sam Turner here. Is this Dr. Martínez?"

"Oh, yes. Hello, Mr. Turner. I was hoping you would call."

"Sharon told me all about the Chávez case. I've always wanted to tackle that school board," he added with a chuckle.

"Thank you so much, Mr. Turner."

"Call me, Sam. And you're the one who should be thanked. Give me the date, time, and address of the board meeting."

"It's on Thursday at 7:00 p.m. at the Superintendent of Schools' conference room on Serra Drive."

"Got it. I'll see you there."

"Thank you again, Sam. I'll let the Chávez family know you're coming." As I hung up the receiver, I felt the same sense of excitement that I had felt back in the '60s.

SIX
Ms. Martínez

Two days later, I found myself rushing through dinner and hurrying out the door in order to arrive at the school board meeting on time. The night before, I had called Mr. and Mrs. Chávez to tell them about Sam. They had thanked me, telling me immediately that they didn't have any money to pay him. But I had reassured them that Sam was donating his services.

My neck felt stiff as I pulled out of the driveway. Today had been exhausting. Client after client—burned-out professors, burned-out mothers. Maybe Frank was right. I needed a break. Listening to people's problems day in and day out was starting to get to me.

As I drove into the parking lot, I recognized the Chávezes' brown station wagon parked in the corner. Good. They were punctual. I waved at them, hurried out of the car, and walked over to where they were standing. I introduced myself in Spanish to Mr. Chávez and politely shook his hand. When I asked him how he was feeling, he told me how nervous they all felt. I tried to put him at ease, telling him that there was nothing to be nervous about.

Then I said hello to Juanita, noticing how pretty she looked. She was dressed very modestly in a blue knee-length dress, and her long black hair was pulled back with a matching barrette.

Out of the corner of my eye, I spotted a group of men and women walking toward the conference room at the corner of the building. I glanced at my watch, reassuring Mr. and Mrs. Chávez that Sam would be here any minute. I reminded them that the school board would have an interpreter present so that they would be able to understand everything that was being said.

Suddenly, I noticed a small red car pulling into the parking lot. It had to be Sam. Mrs. Chávez whispered something that I couldn't understand to her husband. We all stared as a short, gray-haired man with a black briefcase got out of the car and walked over to meet us.

"Hello," I began. "You must be Sam Turner. I'm Sandra Martínez. This is Mr. Chávez, Mrs. Chávez, and their daughter Juanita."

Sam held out his hand to greet Mr. and Mrs. Chávez, and with a warm smile said, *"Buenas tardes."* Mr. Chávez grinned and they shook hands. Then Sam turned to look directly at Juanita. "Hello, young lady. We're going to be seeing a lot of each other in the months to come."

"Hi, Mr. Turner," Juanita said.

"You can call me Sam. Everyone calls me Sam. Even my dog. Just don't call me Sammy, okay?" he said with a wink. Juanita smiled at him. I knew that she was going to like him. "Let's go," he added. "I'm ready for them." We all turned and followed Sam toward the conference room.

I felt my stomach muscles begin to tighten as

we filed into the room. There was a long conference
table at the front of the room where the board
members were seated. There was a microphone in
the middle of the table and a name plate for each of
the board members. I recognized Mr. Jones, the
Dean of Students, sitting next to the principal of
Roosevelt High School.

If I had ever felt like a "Mexican," it was now. I
remembered another school board room, another
high school. I was a senior in college, working
part-time at the local high school as a tutor to the
minority students who were dropping out of school
in large numbers. I had wanted to take my kids to
visit the university so that they could meet some of
my Chicano professors, hoping this would inspire
them. The principal had ordered me to go before
the school board for permission. When I did, they
had all laughed at the idea, and the superintendent
had asked me, "Is it really realistic to think that
these kids will ever get to college?" Fourteen years
later, those words still haunted me. I wondered if
things really had changed.

Sam's voice interrupted my thoughts. He was
instructing us to sit down at the conference table
directly across from the board members, where the
interpreter was already seated. Sam was the first
one to sit down, then Juanita. I sat down next and
told Mr. and Mrs. Chávez to sit by me so that they
would be next to the interpreter. As soon as we sat
down, the interpreter introduced herself to us.

The president of the school board was Dr.
Larson, a thin, balding man with glasses. I
watched closely as he pulled the microphone
toward him and began to speak. Sam whispered to
me that the usual school-board business would

come first. The interpreter was busily translating
everything that was being said for Mr. and Mrs.
Chávez. I noticed that Juanita was nervously twist-
ing a strand of hair that had escaped from her
ponytail.

After about twenty minutes of discussion
among the various board members, Dr. Larson stated that it was time to get into new business. "Next,
we have before us what appears to be a typical
expulsion case. You each have before you a copy of
the expulsion letter that was sent to the Chávez
family. Everyone in favor of the expulsion, please
raise your hand."

Just as quickly as Dr. Larson had called for a
vote from the board members, Sam stood up and, in
an intimidating voice, demanded to be heard. "Wait
a minute here. What happened to due process? My
name is Sam Turner and I have been retained by
the Chávez family to represent Juanita Chávez in
this expulsion case. Although it appears that the
school board has already made its decision, I am
requesting a continuation since I have been just
now retained by the family."

I noticed that Dr. Larson's face had turned
pink, and that several of the board members were
whispering to one another. Appearing very flus-
tered, Dr. Larson took off his glasses, glanced at his
watch, and said, "Well, Mr. Turner, this is a little
out of procedure, but I see no problem with your
proposal. Mr. Turner is requesting a continuation
of the Juanita Chávez expulsion hearing. Everyone
in favor, please raise your hand." The board members reluctantly raised their hands.

"Request granted for continuation," stated Dr.
Larson. "Mr. Turner, we'll see you at next month's

board meeting. This meeting is adjourned."

Sam turned to look at Juanita and said, "Now we have some work to do, young lady. You too, Dr. Martínez."

"Nice work, Sam," I blurted out. I felt in awe of this short little man with the powerful voice. I knew I had a lot to learn from him, and that this would be an experience I would never forget.

Feeling confident again, I turned to Mr. and Mrs. Chávez and explained that the meeting had ended and that we were free to go. The interpreter was already leaving the room, immersed in conversation with several of the board members.

SEVEN
Juanita

It was scary being in that room with all those people, so scary that I thought I was going to pee in my pants. I felt like everyone was staring at me. I hate it when people stare at me. I'm so glad Ms. Martínez was there next to me. And Sam, too. He seems really nice, like he really cares about me.

I could hardly understand what they were saying, all those fancy words. It made me so nervous just hearing them talk. And the school principal kept smiling at me, making me feel so guilty. I don't know why I ever got into a fight with Sheena. It was all so stupid. Now I'll probably never go back to school. Guess I'll just be a dummy.

Why did I let myself get so mad? I should learn to control my temper. I should have just ignored Sheena. Now she's in school and I'm not. Guess I'll just become a vegetable like Maya says, sitting around watching cartoons with the three little ones.

I wonder what Maya is doing right this minute? I wonder if she's thinking about me? She's in fourth period by now. The bell just finished ringing. I wonder who she'll share her lunch with today? Probably Rina. Or maybe they'll all walk

over to the 7-Eleven and get something to eat. I
wish I was there.

I'm so stupid. Why did I let Sheena get to me?
That dumb Carlos. It's all his fault. Why did he go
out with her in the first place? Maybe if he hadn't,
I'd still be in school. Why do I have to have an older
brother anyway? He gets on my nerves, always
bugging me. But I guess this morning he was kinda
nice to me, didn't even call me *fea*, ugly, once. Guess
he felt sorry for me.

I just know everyone at school is talking about
me. Why did this have to happen to me? It's so
awful being home all day. 'Amá keeps finding
things for me to do and I'm sick of cleaning. I'm
sick of her dumb soap operas. This morning when
she was watching *"Rosa Salvaje,"* she started to cry
when Rosa finally finds her son Robertico. I
laughed out loud. I couldn't help it. It's so stupid to
cry for a dumb *novela*.

I wish I could go backwards and undo everything. No fight. No school board meeting. But I
guess I'm just dreaming. Guess I'll just have to get
used to being home with 'Amá. At least Markey is
happy I'm home all day. He loves to play with me.
But even that gets boring after a few days. I wonder what Maya is thinking right now? I wonder if
she has tennis practice today? I wonder if she
misses me?

EIGHT
Juanita

I'm feeling so bored and lonely today. A whole week has gone by since I was kicked out of school. I wonder if they'll ever let me back in school again. I'm sitting down watching cartoons with Markey and my two little sisters when Maya pokes her head through the screen door.

"Hola, Señora Chávez," she yells into the dining room where my 'Amá is folding clothes. "Hi, Johnny. Can I come in?"

"Yeah," I answer as Maya steps inside. She walks over to Markey and ruffles his hair. "Wanna go upstairs?" I ask quickly before she has time to sit down and play with Markey. Maya loves playing with my little brother. Sometimes I have to drag her away from him.

"Sure. See you later, Markey," Maya says as we head for the stairs.

We sit down on the bed and I watch with envy as Maya crosses her long, shapely legs. No wonder the boys are always whistling at her.

"Sorry I haven't come by, but I've been real busy with tennis practice. How's it going? It must be fun being home."

"I hate it. It's so boring. I wish I were back in

school. All I do is clean and watch Markey."

"How was the school board meeting? Bet you were real scared."

"I was really nervous. But it wasn't too bad."

"What do you think of Ms. Martínez? Isn't she cool?"

"Yeah. She's real nice, and pretty, too."

"My mom said you guys took a lawyer with you."

"Yeah. His name is Sam. He's white, but he's real nice. I hope he makes them let me go back to school. Sometimes I think I'll probably never go back to Roosevelt again."

"Don't be a *pendis*," Maya tells me, uncrossing her legs and leaning back against the headboard. Maya likes to make up her own words in Spanish. She calls it Chicano talk. She always calls me a *pendis* when I say something dumb. It's short for *pendeja*.

"I heard Ms. Martínez tell my mom that Sam's a big shot, that he was a big attorney in civil rights cases. I'm sure he'll show them how unfair they're being, kicking you out and not doing anything to Sheena. That's bull."

Maya's words always seem to make me feel stronger. "I know. Just 'cause she's white, they didn't do anything to her. Even Sam said that's not fair."

"When is the next meeting?" Maya asks.

"Not 'til next month. But Ms. Martínez called me and told me that I need to meet with her and Sam in a few weeks."

Maya sits up and crosses her legs again. "Hey, would you like to go to the Rock with me next weekend?"

"The Rock?" I repeat.

"Yes, dummy, the Rock. It's teen night on Thursday."

"Gee, I don't know. 'Apá is so strict, he won't let me go anywhere. I know 'Amá would, but not 'Apá."

"I know what you mean," said Maya. "My dad had a major cow when I first asked him if I could go, but my mom explained to him that there's no liquor, only dancing, and he finally gave in on the condition that he drive me over and pick me up. Aren't parents weird?"

"You're so lucky, Maya. Your parents let you go everywhere. The only way I could go is if I tell 'Apá I'm going to the football game. You'd have to come over and ask him if I could go with you." My mind is racing ahead. I'm already busy planning out the whole thing in my head. It's risky, but I've always wanted to go to the Rock, see what a real college hangout looks like.

"Sure. That's cool," Maya says, changing the subject. "Don't you think Tyrone is handsome? I think he's a doll. He was flirting with me today at lunchtime."

"Was Rudy with him?" I ask. "I think he's cute."

"Which Rudy? The *cholo*?" Maya says, laughing. She's teasing about Rudy's trying to look and act cool.

"Shut up, Maya," I tell her. "Rudy's not a *cholo*. He just dresses like one." Now we both start to laugh. After a minute, Maya glances at the clock radio on my dresser and stands up.

"Listen, I better call my mom at her office so she can come by and pick me up. I'll be right back."

I watch Maya as she leaves the room, wishing I were more like her. She's always so sure of herself. Me, I'm just a dummy. Maya's always right. Maybe Sam and Ms. Martínez will help make everything right again.

I start to bite my nails, a bad habit I started this year. Suddenly, I hear Maya shouting at me, "Stop that, Juanita." And she hits me on the hand, sitting down next to me. Sometimes Maya makes me so mad. She can be so bossy. I guess that's 'cause she's used to getting her way. I bet she's spoiled rotten at her house.

"Come on, Juanita. Stop it," Maya orders me. "I'm going to do your nails with this new polish I just bought." Maya reaches into her bag and pulls out a bottle of shiny purple polish.

We're listening to the radio and doing our nails when we hear someone honking. Maya gets up and looks out the window. "It's my mom. I'll call you later about the Rock. Gotta go."

Downstairs, Maya yells, *"Adios, señora,"* to my mother. Then she races out the door.

I wave goodbye to her from the screen door. Then I sit down to watch cartoons with Rosario and Lupita. Celia gives me a dirty look and tells me it's my turn to help 'Amá with dinner. I ignore her. Markey drops his toy and comes over to me so that I can pick him up. His pants are wet. I'll never understand why Maya thinks I'm so lucky.

NINE
Juanita

On Sunday morning, 'Apá comes bursting into our bedroom hollering at us to get out of bed, that it's time to go to church. I yell at Celia that it's time to wake up and I start to get dressed. 'Apá never goes to church with us, Carlos either. He gets to sleep late. I guess 'Apá thinks only women and children need to go to church. 'Amá says that's the way it is in Mexico. But we don't go to church every Sunday, maybe every other week. 'Amá likes to go to the ten o'clock mass because it's in Spanish, and she can understand what the father is saying. I don't know any prayers in Spanish. I used to when I was little, but not anymore.

After I'm dressed, I help my little sisters get ready. I comb Rosario's hair first and then Lupita's. Their hair is always tangled and they scream every time I touch them. Then we all go downstairs to the kitchen where 'Amá has breakfast waiting for us. 'Apá is sitting in the living room watching T.V. He likes to watch the soccer games on the Spanish station. In Mexico, they call it *fútbol*, but it's really soccer. I think it's a boring sport, but he's crazy about it.

Markey is already at the table eating his oatmeal. Celia is always the last one to come downstairs. She spends forever in front of the mirror, blow-drying her hair. I guess that's how eighth graders act.

When we're all finished eating, we pile into the old station wagon, or the *perrera* as my dad calls it. I get to sit in front with 'Amá since I'm the oldest. This really makes Celia mad. I can hardly wait to get my license. 'Amá drives like a turtle. She just learned how to drive this year, so I guess she's kinda scared. 'Amá doesn't like to go very far in the car because she can't read the signs in English. She only drives to the grocery store and downtown. 'Apá always teases her that someday she'll get lost and won't find her way home. 'Amá just laughs, but I think she really worries about it and that's why she drives like a little old lady. She never gets on the freeway.

The church is already filled with people when we walk in, so we sit in the back. I look around me to see if there are any cute guys, but I don't see any. I recognize a few of my 'Apá's friends. The three little ones love going to church. They think it's fun. I hate it, so does Celia. Markey always has to go *pipí* during the mass, but today he's good. I try to listen to what the father is saying, but I always end up daydreaming. I think about Maya, about school. I wonder what Ms. Martínez is doing this morning.

After the mass has ended, we wait for everyone to leave. Then we follow 'Amá to the front of the church and around the corner to the little room where the statue of the *Virgen de Guadalupe* is waiting for us. 'Amá always lights a candle to her. She's the brown holy Virgin of Mexico who does miracles. 'Amá says that if you pray to her and ask her for something, she always helps you. From the time I was a little girl, 'Amá would tell us stories of how the *Virgen de Guadalupe* made miracles happen. Once 'Amá told me how when her father was very sick in Mexico and she thought he was going to die, 'Amá made a promise to the *Virgen* that she would quit smoking if he were cured. My grandpa got better.

I decide to light a candle with my mother. Maybe the Virgin will help me, too. Maybe she'll make everything right.

✎ ✐ ✎

When we get home, 'Apá and Carlos are waiting for us. Since Sunday is the only day 'Apá doesn't have to work in the fields, he likes to take us to Lake San Martin. Sometimes his friends go with us, but today we're going alone. Carlos and 'Apá have already packed the cooler with sodas and food to barbecue. 'Apá loves to barbecue. It's the only time he cooks. 'Amá says that in Mexico, men don't cook or clean house.

It takes about an hour to drive from our apartment to the lake. This time Carlos gets to sit in front with 'Apá and 'Amá since he's the oldest. Celia and I sit in the back with the three little ones, who are very hyper. They love going to the lake. Carlos acts real grown-up and bossy when he's around 'Apá. It makes me sick, but I just ignore him.

At the lake, we find a nice place to park by one of the picnic tables. The three little ones jump out the back of the station wagon and start running around. Celia and I help 'Amá unpack. Then

Carlos, Celia, and I take off by ourselves to go swimming. The funny thing is that we don't even know how to swim. We just love to get in the water and splash each other.

'Amá watches the three little ones while we swim, and 'Apá sits down to drink a beer and listen to his *norteñas* on the Mexican radio station. He never fishes. He just sits there drinking beer and talking to 'Amá.

Carlos and I team up against Celia, and we splash her so much that she starts crying. We both laugh at her and call her a cry baby. She yells at us and takes off to go tell 'Apá. Sometimes it's fun having a big brother. Sometimes I really like Carlos.

By the time we get out of the water, 'Apá has already started the fire. We're allowed to drink a soda while the food is cooking. Everyone is starving by now, and we can hardly wait to taste 'Apá's hamburgers and hot dogs. I really love going to Lake San Martin. It is the only time we're all together having fun.

About five in the afternoon, it starts to get cooler so we head back to town. The three little ones always fall asleep on the way home. As soon as we get home, Celia and I run upstairs to shower. Carlos gets stuck with helping 'Apá unload the car.

✎   ✏   ✐

Later that evening, I get a call from Ms. Martínez. She asks me how I've been doing. I tell her what a good day I had at the lake. Then Ms. Martínez tells me that she wants me to see her in her office for another meeting. I start to feel nervous again, and I wish I were back at the lake, swimming and laughing with Carlos.

TEN
Ms. Martínez

It was the same dream again. I was standing on the dirt road in front of the old farmhouse. I saw myself peer inside one of the windows. The house looked exactly the same, the big living room with the black coal-burning stove, the cold wooden floors we used to play on. I saw my old room, the bed covered with dolls and the stuffed animals my grandmother would get me from the Salvation Army. I watched myself quietly sneak through the large closet until I found myself in my brother Andy's room. He was lying on the bed asleep, but I couldn't see him because he had the covers pulled up over his face. I tiptoed quietly to his side, but I still couldn't see his face so I slowly started to pull the covers down. I heard myself scream loudly when I saw the fat, grey mice crawling all over his rotting face. I screamed again and again until I suddenly woke up and realized that I had been dreaming.

Yes. It was only a dream, I thought to myself. Another of those awful dreams. I felt the daylight pouring in through the window. Me and my silly dreams. I always dreamt more when I was tired.

I reached over to feel for Frank, but he wasn't there. I looked at the alarm clock and saw the note that he had left me: "Had to leave early. Just remember how much I love you, Sandy. Don't overdo it." God, Frank was so good to me. So thoughtful. What would I ever do without him? How he put up with all of this was beyond me: the endless phone calls, the neurotic patients.

I remembered last night's call. It had been Beth calling me at one in the morning. Poor Beth, all strung out on pills since her husband had left her with a minimum-wage job and two small kids to support. I had tried to calm her down, promising to meet her in my office first thing this morning.

Frank was probably used to all of this by now. No choice. But lately he had been nagging me more than usual about how tired I was looking, how I should slow down and not see so many patients. Maybe he was right. I was beginning to feel the strain, to get sick of it all. Sick of listening to everyone else's problems day after day. I was beginning to think I needed a shrink myself.

The ringing of the telephone interrupted my thoughts. I sat up, reaching for the receiver.

"Hello."

"Sandy, is that you?"

Panic began to set in. It was my mother. That was the last thing I needed. "Yes, Mom. How's it going?"

"Well, your dad and I have been worried because we haven't heard from you. Are you all right?"

It was just like my mother to worry about every little thing. "I'm fine, mom, just been real busy, that's all." I knew she wouldn't believe me.

"Well, I wish you'd call once in a while and let us know you're alive."

I let out a small laugh, knowing well that this would irritate her. I could feel her frustration through the telephone.

"I just wanted to know if you were coming to visit us for Thanksgiving. We'd really like it if you came. Your *tía* Luisa is going to be here."

"I'm not sure if I can, mom. I'm super busy at work." Somehow my mother always knew when I was making an excuse.

"Is it because of Frank? Ever since you married him, it seems like you hardly come see us."

God, I hated this. Here I was, almost forty, and she was still trying to run my life. I hated that. "No, Mom. It has nothing to do with Frank. He always enjoys going over there. I'm just very busy at the office."

"Sandy, every time I talk to you, you sound so tired. Are you taking the right vitamins?" My mother was on some kind of vitamin kick these days.

"Yes, Mom," I answered.

"Well, your Dad and I would really like it if you came, okay?"

How could I tell her how much I hated going back there. Nothing ever seemed to change in that dead town. Same run-down buildings, same old faces. And all that pain, those haunting memories still alive, waiting to engulf me.

"Tell Frank we want to see you, okay, Sandy? Don't let him talk you into going to L. A. to his parents' instead."

She had always resented my marrying Frank. The day I had told her that we were getting married, she had said, "To a *gabacho*? Why can't you marry one of our kind?" And from the first time she had met

Frank, she never ceased to point out everything that was wrong with him, from his hairline to his old sneakers. I hadn't even bothered to invite her to the wedding, but she had just showed up anyway, looking miserable among Frank's family.

"Mom, I have to go or I'll be late for my appointments. I'll call you later," I said, hanging up quickly before she could respond. Twenty minutes later, I had showered and dressed. I sat down at the kitchen table with an English muffin and a cup of black coffee to look over my day's schedule. My first appointment wasn't until ten. Good. Beth would be waiting for me when I got there and I would have time for her. Next, Mrs. Gray. Then lunch with Sonia at the little Chinese restaurant. It was her turn to treat. Good, I didn't need to run by the pocket teller. The afternoon looked pretty busy, a couple of students I had just started seeing, then Juanita at four o'clock. I would be ready for a change by then, after listening to white people's problems all day long. Besides, I liked Juanita. She reminded me so much of myself at that age, young, scared and angry. Angry at the whole world and not able to express it. Maybe I could help her. Maybe I could save Juanita.

The morning went smoothly. Beth had come and gone, and Mrs. Gray had been feeling pretty optimistic for a change. Sonia cancelled on me so I took a leisurely walk across the street to the little hamburger place on the corner. I sat outside and ate my greasy burger, thinking how good it felt to have a relaxing morning for a change. It was a sunny day and the sun felt good on my face.

A half-hour later, I was back in my office. By the time four o'clock rolled around, my head ached and my voice was hoarse from talking. I needed some aspirin. I got up and went out to the small kitchen for a glass of water.

As I swallowed my two aspirins, I heard the buzzer ring at the front desk. I hurried out to the reception area, knowing it would be Juanita. I spotted her right away. "Hello, Juanita. How are you?" I asked.

"Hi, Ms. Martínez," Juanita answered with a smile that let me know she was really glad to see me. She didn't seem as nervous today. Maybe it was the fact that she was dressed in jeans and sneakers.

"No mother today?"

"No. I walked over by myself this time."

"It's a great day for walking. Well, follow me, young lady.

Juanita followed me straight to my office. She sat down on the old couch, in the same spot as before.

"How have you been doing, Juanita?" I asked, breaking the momentary silence.

"Better, I guess."

"That's great."

"Well, not that good," Juanita said. "I just, you know, feel a little better, but I really miss school a lot."

"I have some news that will make you feel better. Sam is contacting the school so that they can give you home tutoring. He said you're entitled to it until we get you back in school."

Juanita's eyes widened and a smile lit up her face. "Really, Ms. Martínez? That would be good 'cause I don't want to get too far behind in my school work."

"Well, don't worry. We won't let that happen. How are things at home?"

I had to be careful not to intimidate her with my questions.

"Fine, I guess. A little boring." Juanita lowered her eyes and began playing with a strand of hair that had fallen over her cheek. I could tell that it was going to be difficult getting her to open up today.

I waited a few minutes, hoping Juanita would say something, and when she didn't, I decided to take the lead. "I thought you were really brave at the school board meeting. I know how hard it must have been for you, being the only student there with all those adults."

Juanita looked up at me. "Yeah, I felt really scared. I felt like the principal was giving me dirty looks the whole time."

"Well, Sam and I were impressed at how well you handled yourself. The next meeting will be even easier because you'll know what to expect."

Silence. More silence. I was getting ready to say something when she looked up at me and asked me a question I hadn't anticipated.

"Were your parents very strict with you, Ms. Martínez?"

"You mean when I was your age, Juanita?"

"Yeah," Juanita answered, looking down at her sneakers.

"Boy, were they ever strict," I said, noticing that she was looking at me again. "I couldn't go anywhere. They wouldn't let me date until I was eighteen." I thought back to my high school years. The constant lies, sneaking out windows with my cousins to meet boys. And Raúl. My sweet, young

Raúl. Juanita's voice brought me back from the past.

"My dad, well, he's the boss of the house and he's so strict with me and Celia. He won't let us talk to guys on the phone and he won't let us date at all until we're little old ladies, I guess."

Now I had Juanita's complete attention and I could tell that she was beginning to trust me. "And how does that make you feel?" I asked, knowing that I was beginning to sound like a shrink again.

"Well, its kinda hard 'cause everyone in school dates already. I feel like I'm the only one who can't." Juanita paused for a moment, looking out the window and then turned to me and said, "And this week Maya wants me to go to teen night with her at this dance club, and I guess I'll just have to lie to my parents."

"What happens if you get caught lying, Juanita? Have you thought about the consequences?" I asked, thinking back once more to my own teenage years. I had never cared about consequences, only about Raúl. Even that awful night when my mother had caught me sneaking in at two in the morning, I still hadn't cared.

"Well, I don't know, Ms. Martínez. But I've decided to go with Maya," Juanita answered very matter-of-factly.

"Is it that important to you, Juanita?" I asked, knowing that this was a stupid question. Of course it was important.

"It's just that I want to be like everyone else. I hate being treated like a baby. Everyone at school thinks it's weird that I can't date yet."

"Why is it so important what everyone at school thinks?"

"Well, I don't know. It's just that I want to be like everyone else."

I knew that this was the perfect moment to bring up the fight. "Juanita, I'd like for us to talk about fighting in school, because I'm sure that the board members will want to know how you feel about that." I watched her closely to see how she would react. She started to gaze out the window again.

After a few minutes, Juanita spoke. "It was wrong. I know it was. I lost my temper and it won't happen again." A hurt look appeared on Juanita's face. I knew that she needed me as much as I needed her.

"Maybe we can come up with some alternatives to fighting, Juanita. For example, if someone were to start bothering you at school again and wanted to fight, what could you do to avoid a fight? You said Sheena pushed you first, right? Well, what if another person comes up to you and pushes you. What can you do instead of getting into a physical fight?"

Juanita didn't answer me right away. I waited patiently while she came up with her own solution. After a few minutes, Juanita told me, "I guess I could walk away. Or go find a teacher and tell them about it."

"Good thinking, Juanita. But what if your friends call you a chicken?"

"Then I guess they're not my real friends."

"That's absolutely right, Juanita. Your friends wouldn't want you to get hurt. It's also very important to talk with someone about your feelings. It isn't good to keep them bottled up inside until you burst open. Is there anyone at school or at home that you can talk to?" I asked, knowing that I was beginning to probe deeper into the problem.

"Not really. I hate those counselors at school. They act like they don't care. And the teachers, well, I don't know any of them very good. I'd be embarrassed to talk to them."

I understood only too well what Juanita meant. God, it seemed like things never changed, the same problems, the same attitudes. I felt like I was back where I had started many, many years ago. Yet, I knew I couldn't give up.

"How about friends at school?" I asked. "Do you talk to Maya about your feelings?"

"Sometimes. She's my best friend."

"I'm so glad that you have a friend like Maya. I know she really likes you. I'd like to be your friend too, Juanita. I'd really like it if you kept coming to see me for the rest of the school year. What do you think?"

Her face lit up with a smile. "I'd like that, too, Ms. Martínez."

I reached over and hugged her, feeling good about myself again, about life and about my profession. Not everything was lost after all.

ELEVEN
Ms. Martínez

That entire week, I couldn't keep Juanita out of my thoughts. It felt good to feel useful again, to feel like my career had a purpose to it. I felt exhilarated, a feeling I hadn't experienced in quite some time, and I looked forward to my next meeting with Juanita. Sam had telephoned me on Thursday night, asking me to arrange a meeting at my house on Saturday so that he could get the information he needed from Juanita before the next board meeting. Sam said that it was best to meet at my house instead of his office so that Juanita would feel more comfortable.

On Saturday morning, I awoke to the smell of fresh coffee and bacon. I dressed quickly and hurried out to the kitchen.

"Hi, hon. Did you sleep well?" Frank asked.

"Oh, you're so sweet. Why didn't you wake me?" I answered, giving him a short kiss on the lips.

"Oh, do that again," Frank said jokingly. "You were so tired last night that I thought I'd let you sleep in. Now sit down, everything is ready."

I watched Frank lovingly as he poured me a cup of coffee. He was definitely the best thing that had

ever happened to me, so tender and thoughtful.
Always helping me with everything. I had never met
a man who washed dishes and did laundry. Frank
was amazing. Sometimes I felt embarrassed when my
parents visited and saw Frank helping with the
housework. In the Mexican and Chicano cultures,
only women did housework. I knew my mother dis-
approved.

"This is wonderful," I told him as he devoured
a huge pile of bacon. Frank loved to eat. Sometimes
I enjoyed just sitting back and watching him savor
every mouthful. It was a good thing that Frank
was naturally thin like his father and didn't have
to worry about getting fat. "Where are you off to
this morning?" I asked between mouthfuls, wishing
I could eat like him and not worry about my
weight.

"I need to go into the office today to finish up
some work. Then I thought I'd go to the gym if
that's all right with you."

"Only if you promise to come home early so
that we can spend the rest of the afternoon together. Sam and Juanita will be here at ten, and we
should be finished by noon. Then I guess I'll lounge
around the house, maybe watch some T. V."

"That sounds good to me," Frank said, gulping
down his last mouthful. "I'll promise to come back
early." He glanced at his watch. "Well, hon, guess I
better run. Now promise me you'll take time to
relax today."

"Of course I will. Don't worry so much. Are you
sure you got enough to eat?" I asked, smiling.

Frank laughed and came around the table to
kiss me, running his hand down my blouse. "I'm
still hungry. What did you have in mind?"

I laughed out loud. "Frank, you dirty old man. Work first, play later."

"Slave driver," he told me, kissing me again and heading for the front door. As he left, I heard him singing, "Come on, baby, light my fire. Try to set the night on fire."

I smiled to myself. Frank was such a clown. So different from Raúl, from any man I'd ever known. I mustn't think about Raúl now.

I got up from the table and started loading the dishwasher. Then I poured myself another cup of coffee and went into the living room to relax.

Half an hour later, the doorbell rang. I put my newspaper down and walked over to answer the door, knowing it would be either Sam or Juanita. It was Sam.

"Come in, Sam. How are you?"

"Hello, Sandy. Well, it could be better. Is Juanita here yet?" he asked, sitting down in the nearest armchair.

"She should be arriving any minute."

"Oh, she's running on Mexican time. I forgot about that. You know us *gringos*, always punctual," Sam said with a twinkle in his eye. We both laughed. "How are the counselling sessions coming along?" he asked.

"We're doing great. Juanita is beginning to trust me and she has agreed to meet with me every two weeks."

"That's good news, Sandy, because if we can show the school board that Juanita is getting rehabilitated, that will help our case. You know how *gringos* think. They love it when people are rehabilitated."

I had to laugh. Sam certainly knew something

about cultural differences.

"Sandy, you have to know the *gringo* system well in order to fight it. They get totally shaken up when they see a white person like me on the other side."

"Yes, I noticed that at the first meeting. They totally ignored me, but your presence really rattled them."

"That's because I know how they think," Sam told me.

The doorbell rang. "That must be Juanita," I said. I went over to the front door and opened it. Juanita was standing on the doorstep holding a large bag filled with vegetables.

"Hi, Ms. Martínez. These are for you. My dad works at the farm and he brought these for you."

"That was very nice of him," I told Juanita, taking the bag from her hands. "Sam is already here. Come on in."

As soon as Juanita had stepped inside, Sam stood up to greet her. "Hello, young lady."

"Hi, Mr. Turner, I mean Sam," Juanita answered shyly.

"Juanita, sit down and talk to Sam while I take these into the kitchen. Can I get you anything to drink?"

"No, thanks, Ms. Martínez. I'm fine," Juanita answered, sitting on the couch next to Sam.

"We've got a lot of work to do, young lady," Sam told her, opening his briefcase. "I've brought my tape recorder with me today. Now don't let that make you nervous, okay? It's easier for me to record our conversation instead of trying to write down everything from memory. You know us old people can't remember anything."

Juanita grinned. "That's okay. I don't mind."

I came back into the living room and sat next to Juanita. I knew that telling Sam all about the fight wouldn't be easy.

"Okay," Sam said. "Let's get started. I want you to tell me how the fight started. I'll need for you to think clearly and be as accurate as you can."

"I'll do my best," Juanita answered. I noticed that she was beginning to twirl a strand of hair, round and round. I patted her on the shoulder, letting her know that I was right here to help her. Going back was always painful.

TWELVE
Juanita

"Sheena and I have had our differences. We talked off and on before the fight. This last summer she started telling rumors about me. You see, she was dating my brother Carlos and he broke up with her and she kept bugging us on account of Carlos. He didn't want to date her no more. So she kept saying bad things about me and my family. She kept passing by our house during the week. Sometimes when I saw her, she'd yell things at me. She told my sister Celia that I was no virgin, that I was a "bitch" and a "ho." And she told my friend, Rina Acevedo, the same thing. I also read a letter she wrote behind Rina's back saying bad things about Blacks. Rina saw the letter and got upset. I know Sheena's prejudiced. Well, I wanted to find out why Sheena was saying all those bad things, so I confronted Sheena with all of this and she denied it. Then Sheena told me that she did tell my sister those things because she was mad at me. So that's how everything started.

"Then in September sometime, she was in the lockers, the girls' P.E. lockers. We were getting dressed for P.E. and Sheena was telling the girls that she knew everyone's credits. Then she looked

64

at me and said, 'I know how much credits you have.' I told her not to tell me because I knew how much credits I had. Then she said, 'Well, I work in the office so I know you're thirty credits behind.' I was embarrassed even though I didn't know some of the girls around me. So my reply was that I was going to graduate. Then Sheena said, 'I'm going to graduate on stage.' I said, 'Sheena, everyone graduates on stage.' Sheena said, 'No, not everyone graduates on stage. Look at your family.' I was very hurt. Then I said, 'Why are you bringing my family into this? Don't use my family as an example.' She didn't say anything. Then I told her I was going to tell my brother what she said. Sheena said, 'Go ahead or I'll tell him before you do.' Later my counselor, Mr. Lant, called me in for a meeting about some night classes. So I told him about Sheena getting into my records. He said she was not supposed to do that and he would talk to her. I figured this was a breach of confidentiality. Sheena was very upset because my brother didn't want to speak to her, and 'cause he wanted to go out with other girls, like Rina. Sheena would go around telling people at school how she wished she could hit me, and that if I fought her I could get into so much trouble. Then she was going around saying that Rina and I were supposed to jump her.

So my intentions the day of the fight were to go up to Sheena and confront her with the bad things she was saying. That day, I was walking up to my P.E. locker and I told my friend Rina that I was scared. She told me that she would come with me. Well, I saw Sheena by her locker and I asked her why she was saying all those lies about me and my family. She started yelling at me, so I felt even

more nervous. I knew that she was not going to
back down. She was looking down at my face,
telling me to hit her. I had no intentions to fight, so
I told her I was not going to hit her. Then Sheena
told me that if I did hit her, she could get me put in
juvenile hall. The bell rang and she was getting
even more aggressive, yelling at me. So I decided to
stick up for myself. Then Sheena pushed me. I
grabbed her and she grabbed my hair and started
punching me. So I did the same. Then she was
falling and she was bringing me down with her.
Her head banged into the bench. She was trying to
get on top of me. I was tired and I wanted to stop,
but she had both legs wrapped around my waist so
I couldn't get loose. I pushed her head back twice
and she kept punching my face. So we were both
punching each other in the face. A bunch of girls
were already around us. I didn't know she was
bleeding. Then the P.E. teacher, Mrs. Allen, came
and told us to stop. I was getting up and Sheena
hit me, so I hit her back. Mrs. Allen grabbed my
hand and started accusing me. Sheena was standing up in the crowd crying. Then she went back
down to her knees. She was letting some loud sobs
out. Some of the girls were trying to calm her
down. Then Mrs. Fellini came and took me to the
Dean of Student's office. Sheena's mom was called
right away and my mom wasn't called 'til about an
hour later. Mr. Jones asked me if there were any
people around watching. I told him there were all
kinds of girls. I tried to tell him everything, but
everything had happened so fast. I couldn't remember all that had been said. He questioned a couple
of students that saw the fight, and he told Rina,
'Do you feel like mostly blacks and Mexicans are

doing the fighting?" He also asked her if she knew if I came from a rough family. I told all of this to my mom. I guess that's how the fight happened. It's hard to remember everything since it happened so fast."

THIRTEEN
Juanita

On Sunday, I get real happy when Maya calls to talk about going to the Rock. I've been feeling so bad since yesterday that it helps to think about something else. It was really hard telling Sam about the fight. I felt so embarrassed. Afterwards, I went home and cried in my room.

By Monday, I start to feel a lot better. That whole week I'm busy thinking about the story I need to invent in order to get permission to go to the dance on Thursday night. I've never lied to my parents before. This makes me feel nervous and afraid. I hate telling lies, but I know that my 'Apá will never give me permission to go to a dance club. 'Amá might, but not 'Apá. Why can't my 'Apá be more like other parents? He's so protective it makes me sick.

On Wednesday evening, I wait until my 'Apá has finished his dinner and is relaxing in front of the T.V. before I talk to him. He gets home real tired after working in the fields all day, so he likes to sit down and watch the eight o'clock *novela* with my 'Amá, the one with Lucía Méndez. He watches every single *novela* Lucía Méndez is in. My 'Amá hates Lucía Méndez. I think she's jealous of her.

I sit down next to 'Apá on the couch, and when a commercial comes on, I start talking about the game. Using my best Spanish, I tell 'Apá that Maya has invited me to go the football game with her on Thursday night. I ask him if I can go. 'Amá is looking at me suspiciously. How is it that mothers always seem to know everything?

'Apá turns away from the T.V. and tells me he's not sure. Then he asks me about all the school work the tutor has given me. I tell him that I'll finish it all before Thursday and that Maya's dad will give me a ride to the game and bring me home again.

'Apá turns to look at the screen again. Lucía Méndez is sobbing, and he whispers, "*Pobrecita.*" Then 'Apá looks at me again. He tells me, "*Está bien,*" and warns me to be home by eleven.

"*Gracias,* 'Apá," I say, kissing him on the cheek and racing back upstairs. Later that night, I call Maya to give her the good news.

✎   ✏   ✐

On Thursday afternoon, I hurry and do all my chores without complaining. By noon, I have finished my schoolwork. I spend the next two hours trying to decide what to wear. When Celia gets home, she starts bugging me by telling me how fat I look in everything I try on. I know that she's jealous 'cause I'm going out and she's not. I finally bribe her with my new polish so that she will leave me alone in the room for a while. Later, I start to worry that Carlos will tell my 'Amá that there is no football game tonight. I'm relieved when he comes home just to change clothes and then leaves with his friends. Finally, I decide to wear my black skirt and red top.

At seven o'clock sharp, Maya comes to pick me up. I can tell she's nervous about lying to my mother 'cause she keeps fidgeting from one foot to the other while she waits for me to get my coat. 'Amá doesn't say anything, but I can tell she's very suspicious.

I get in the back seat with Rina and the three of us giggle all the way downtown. Maya's dad is a lot of fun. He keeps teasing us about gossiping.

When we get to the Rock, Maya's dad reminds us that he'll pick us up in the same spot at exactly 10:45 p.m. Feeling very grown up, we get out of the car and walk over to the entrance.

"They say a lot of college guys come here," Maya says as we line up to pay. "We'll have to check them out."

"I'm really nervous about lying to my parents," I tell Maya and Rina.

"Don't sweat it," says Rina. "I do it all the time. You'll get used to it."

Inside, it's dark and the music is blaring. I love Rap music. I drive my 'Amá crazy with it. All she wants to listen to is her dumb Mexican music. When my eyes adjust to the darkness, I notice that there are tables all around the room. The dance floor is at the front. I can see groups of guys and girls sitting at different tables. We giggle nervously 'cause we have never been to a real dance club before.

"Look, there's Tyrone with Tommy and Rudy!" Rina squeals.

"Shut up," Maya tells her, and we pretend not to notice them as we follow Maya over to the nearest empty table. We sit down, noticing that the refreshment bar is behind us.

"Too bad we can't get a beer," says Maya.

"That would be cool," adds Rina.

"*Están locas*," I scold them. "Let's get a Coke."

We walk over to the refreshment bar and order a soda. We're getting ready to pay when Tommy walks up to us, "Hey, what's happening? How's it going, Johnny? I heard about the school board meeting and all that stuff."

Before I have time to answer him, Tommy grabs Rina's Coke and Maya yells, "*Baboso*," at him. Rina punches him in the arm and he gives back the Coke. We all laugh. Tommy loves to tease us. I don't care what anyone says about him. He's the nicest guy in the whole school. All the other guys try to hit on us. Not Tommy. He's just a good friend.

"Did you come with Tyrone?" I ask Tommy as we head back to our table. Before he can answer me, Maya grabs him by the arm.

"Come on, Tommy, don't be a jerk. Let's dance." Maya hands Rina her Coke and pulls Tommy out to the dance floor. Me and Rina walk back to our table.

Back at our table, Rina tells me, "That Maya is too much."

"Yeah. I wish I could be more like her. She's not afraid of anything," I answer, gazing enviously at the couples on the dance floor.

Ten minutes later, Maya comes back to our table. In an excited voice, she tells us, "I saw Tyrone when I was dancing with Tommy. He just kept staring at me."

"Was Rudy with him?" I ask Maya, trying not to show how excited I really am.

"I think so. Maybe they'll come over and ask us to dance."

The next song begins to play and we sit quietly watching all the couples on the dance floor. A chubby, pimple-faced guy that we've never seen before comes over to ask Rina to dance. We giggle as they walk out to the dance floor. The next thing I know, someone is tapping me on the shoulder. I turn around and meet Rudy's eyes.

"Hey, Johnny, wanna dance?" he asks.

I feel my heart beating rapidly. I've never danced with Rudy before. I feel nervous. What should I do? I turn to look at Maya, but she's walking out to the dance floor with Tyrone. I shouldn't be such a chicken. I should be more like Maya. "Sure," I mumble to Rudy, hoping that I won't step on him while we're dancing and make a fool of myself.

Rudy holds my hand as we walk out to the dance floor. His hand is sweaty, but it sure feels good. We start dancing. I try not to look at Rudy's face. We dance one song after another until I finally start to relax. Then a slow song comes on and Rudy put his arms around me and pulls me close. My heart is beating so fast that I wonder if I'm going to have a heart attack. I've never danced like this with a boy before.

Tyrone and Maya are dancing next to us. It looks like Tyrone is kissing Maya on the cheek. I feel Rudy pulling me closer to him. He smells like Old Spice. I start to feel panicky. What will I do if Rudy tries to kiss me? I've never been kissed by a boy before. I wonder what it feels like. Before I can come up with an answer, the music changes and Rudy lets go of me. We dance a few more dances and then we go back to our table. Tyrone is there, sitting next to Maya. Rina is still on the dance floor. I sit down and Rudy sits next to me.

"Johnny, let's go *pipí*, " Maya tells me and the guys laugh. Feeling embarrassed, I get up quickly and follow Maya to the bathroom. While I wait for Maya, I put on some lipstick and comb my hair. I don't recognize any of the girls in the bathroom. After about a minute, Maya is standing next to me again.

"God, Tyrone is such a hunk."

"So is Rudy," I answer, and we both laugh.

"I wonder if Rina scored," Maya says, brushing her long hair.

"I hope it's not with that fatso," I say, and we start laughing again.

We're walking out of the bathroom when we almost bump into a group of girls. It's Sheena with some of her friends from school.

"Watch where you're going," Sheena says, glaring at me. "I didn't know they let Mexicans in here."

I can feel my face burning. Before I can say anything, Maya puts her arm through mine and tells me, "Just ignore her, Johnny." I feel like I'm about to explode. "Mind your own business, Sheena," I blurt out. Sheena is still glaring at me and I can feel myself getting angrier. Suddenly, I remember Ms. Martínez. I can hear her telling me, "It's important to learn to control your temper, Juanita. You can learn to do it." Ms. Martínez is right. I can do it.

"You're the one who should mind her own business," Sheena yells at me.

I can feel Maya's finger's digging into my arm,

trying to pull me toward our table. I'm getting ready to walk away from Sheena when I suddenly hear my brother's voice coming from behind Sheena.

"Leave her alone, Sheena. She's not bothering anyone," Carlos says, stepping around Sheena. "Juanita, what are you doing here?" Before I can answer, Carlos grabs me by the hand and leads me and Maya out toward the entrance. Carlos stops by the door. "How did you get here, Juanita?"

"I came with Maya," I answer, feeling scared and humiliated.

"Yeah, Carlos. My dad brought us," Maya says in a shaky voice. I can tell that Maya is feeling scared, too.

"Does 'Amá know you're here?" Carlos asks me.

My face is burning hot. I avoid Carlos's eyes. "No. She thinks I went to a game with Maya."

"It's my fault, Carlos. I talked her into it," says Maya. But Carlos ignores her.

"Well, we're going home now. Maya, tell your dad that Juanita went home with me."

Maya mumbles "okay" and starts walking back inside. I follow Carlos out the front door.

"Tonta," Carlos says as we walk towards the parking lot. "See what happens when you lie? What if Sheena had started a fight with you again? She hates our guts."

"I didn't think she'd be there. I wouldn't have gotten into a fight with her anyway."

"It's a good thing I showed up when I did."

"Thanks, Carlos. But please don't tell 'Amá. I'm really sorry for lying."

"I'll think about it, *fea*," he says as we climb

into his friend's car.

I start to feel better. I can tell that Carlos feels sorry for me and wants to help me. Maybe Maya is right. Maybe it is good to have brothers and sisters.

FOURTEEN
Ms. Martínez

"Hon, are you sure you should go tonight?" Frank asked, reaching over to feel my forehead. "I think you have a fever."

"I have to. Juanita needs me there. Anyway, Sam said it would be short and informal," I answered, getting up slowly from the kitchen table. It had been a long, stressful day. Client after client, problem after problem. At one point, I had felt like screaming and telling them all to go away. I felt drained and I was beginning to wonder how much longer I could keep this up. I reached inside the hall closet.

Frank walked over to my side. "Your mother called again. What have you decided about Thanksgiving?" he asked, helping me put on my jacket.

"I'm too exhausted to take a trip. You know that. She'll just have to understand. But you know my mother, she'll have an angry fit. Oh, well, I can't worry about that now. I'll call her later. I really have to go now." I reached over and gave Frank a quick kiss.

"Hon, do you want me to drive you?" Frank asked.

I smiled at him. "I'll be fine. Stop being a fussy old husband."

"You know me. I'm just an old fart."

I laughed, kissing him once more before I walked out the door.

✎ ✏ ✐

When I arrived at the school administration building, Juanita and her parents were already there, standing next to their car talking with Sam. I got out of the car and hurried over to meet them.

"Hello, Sam. Hi, Juanita," I said, trying not to sound fatigued. Then I switched to Spanish and greeted Mr. and Mrs. Chávez. I politely shook hands with Mr. Chávez.

"Let's hurry and go inside, Sandy," Sam said. "They're waiting for us." We turned and followed Sam into the conference room.

Inside, Sam pointed to the same seats we had occupied in the previous meeting. As we sat down, I noticed several new faces across the room that I hadn't seen at the last meeting. Also, the interpreter seemed to be eyeing me suspiciously.

After a few minutes Dr. Larson cleared his voice and began speaking into his microphone.

"The board has convened to hear the proposed disciplinary action against Juanita Chávez. I am Carl Larson, President of the School Board. The Chávez family is represented by Mr. Sam Turner. The nature of this hearing is to hear evidence relative to the charges against Juanita Chávez. Will all the people who intend to speak or testify at this meeting please stand and raise your right hand."

Sam and several of the new people present

stood up, raising their right hands. This was suddenly beginning to sound like a court trial.

"Do each of you swear or affirm that the testimony you may give in this hearing shall be the
truth, the whole truth and nothing but the truth?"
asked Dr. Larson.

Everyone standing repeated, "I do." Then Dr.
Larson instructed them to sit down again. The
interpreter's voice was buzzing away, translating
every word for Mr. and Mrs. Chávez. I noticed that
Juanita was twirling a long strand of hair. She had
every right to feel nervous. I patted her arm gently.

Dr. Larson started to speak again. "At this
time, I would like to introduce Mr. Ted Robbins,
Attorney at Law for the Roosevelt School District.
He will be conducting the hearing today."

I saw Sam jerk his head up. I could tell by the
look on his face that he was as startled as I was. I
leaned across Juanita and whispered to him,
"Didn't they say it would be informal?"

Dr. Larson then turned to Mr. Robbins and
said, "Please state your name before speaking."

"My name is Ted Robbins. I'm the legal counsel
appearing on behalf of the school administration.
This involves an expulsion case concerning one of
the students in your district. Her name is Juanita
Chávez. Miss Chávez has been charged with battery on school grounds this fall. To prove that she
engaged in this misconduct, and to give you the
grounds for dismissal, we are going to call several
witnesses. These witnesses are Mr. Jones, Dean of
Students at Roosevelt High School, and two eyewit-
nesses to the battery, Mrs. Janice Allen and Mrs.
Elizabeth Fellini, both teachers. Now I would like
to call your attention to a document which is in the

packet which was presented before the hearing to the Board. That document appears on pages ten and eleven in the Board's packet. I'd like to ask you to turn to this now."

Feeling horrified, I watched quietly as Sam stood up to protest what was happening. "Dr. Larson, I was not informed of any witnesses nor did I receive copies of any of these documents prior to the meeting."

"Sit down, Mr. Turner," ordered Dr. Larson. "You will have your turn to speak after Mr. Robbins has presented his information. Please continue, Mr. Robbins."

Sam hesitated for a minute before sitting down again. Juanita's head was bowed down. I knew that she was feeling frightened. We all were.

"I would like to call Mr. Jones, Dean of Students. Mr. Jones, have you seen this document before?"

Mr. Jones leaned forward and said, "Yes, I have."

"Are you the author of this document?"

"Yes, I am."

"Would you please read your statement out loud."

Mr. Jones began to read. "On Oct. 11 at approximately 12:10 p.m., student Sheena Martin approached her P.E. teacher, Mrs. Janice Allen, before the start of class, stating that she had been told by several students that Juanita Chávez was going to start a fight with her. Sheena declined to wait in the teacher's office since she thought it might just be a rumor. Shortly after, Juanita approached Sheena in the locker room and an argument began. Neither girl attempted to back down from the argument. The fight began with both students throwing and landing punches.

Sheena and Juanita grabbed each other by the hair and fell to the floor. Juanita then grabbed Sheena by the hair with both hands and repeatedly hit Sheena's head against the concrete floor. Arriving on the scene, Mrs. Allen had to pull Juanita off of Sheena. It was necessary for Juanita to be further restrained by another teacher, Mrs. Elizabeth Fellini. The school nurse examined Sheena and found some bleeding on the back of her head. Sheena was also bleeding from the mouth and had a swollen upper lip. She was transported to the nearest hospital as a precautionary measure."

Sam was standing up again. His face was a dark shade of pink. "May I interrupt here? I'm really alarmed that I didn't know about this report. I don't think it is quite fair to spring this by surprise."

"Mr. Turner, I was informed that this document was given to you. The family was sent a packet by certified mail giving them all this information," said Mr. Robbins.

"I don't know about that. I'm the attorney and I did not know this information existed. If you had sent this information to me, I would have known of it's significance. I don't expect a family who can't read or write English to understand it. I object going any further with this."

"Sit down, Mr. Turner," demanded Dr. Larson. "Mr. Robbins, you may continue."

"Now I would like the school board members to turn to page fifteen of the board's packet. Mr. Jones, are you also the author of this statement?"

"Yes."

"When did you prepare this statement?"

"About two weeks prior to the expulsion hearing."

"Please read the first sentence only, Mr. Jones."

"On September 29, during lunch, an argument ensued between Juanita Chávez and Ann Lant."

"Mr. Jones, what are the facts that support your conclusion in this sentence?" asked Mr. Robbins.

"In interviewing Ann Lant, she indicated that there had been an argument between them at lunchtime," Mr. Jones answered.

Sam was on his feet again. This time he was shouting. "I strongly object to the inclusion of this new information which I have not seen. It has nothing to do with the so-called battery at issue here."

"Dr. Larson, I am attempting to show that Juanita Chávez had a pattern of violent behavior that led to this battery," said Mr. Robbins.

Sam refused to keep quiet. "I don't think you can put a young girl in a hearing like this and not have her counsel adequately prepared. My duty is to make the best case I can for this young woman. I wasn't informed of any witnesses, nor did I get these documents. I don't think it's right to take this young lady and put her through this with inadequately prepared counsel. You can do it if you want to. I can't stop you. But I think it's wrong," Sam shouted, sitting back down.

"To expedite this matter," stated the board president, "I suggest we move on to the actual battery and let the two witnesses testify."

Sam mumbled something that I couldn't make out. I felt just as outraged as he did. Juanita was nervously biting her nails, trying not to look up at anyone.

Mr. Robbins started to speak again. "My first witness is Mrs. Janice Allen, the P.E. teacher at

Roosevelt High School. Would you please state your name and tell us exactly what happened on the afternoon of October 11."

The tall, middle-aged woman sitting next to the Dean of Students began to speak. "My name is Janice Allen. Sheena did come to me before class to tell me that she was afraid that Juanita was going to start a fight with her. I asked her if she had told this to her counselor and she said no. I tried to get Sheena to not dress for P.E. and instead go see her counselor, but she said she would go later. So she insisted on dressing for P.E."

"Did Sheena seem frightened, Mrs. Allen?" asked Mr. Robbins.

"Well, she looked somewhat scared. I told her I would talk to Juanita after class. I thought it might be a rumor, and I didn't want to talk to Juanita about it if it wasn't true. I never thought for a moment a fight would start in the locker room."

"Did you witness the fight?"

"I wasn't there when it began. A couple of students came to get me, and by the time I got there, they were already on the floor fighting."

"Was Juanita on top of Sheena?"

"Yes, she was. I ran over and pulled her off of Sheena."

"Mrs. Allen, is it a fact that Juanita was in a blind rage and you had some difficulty getting her off of Sheena?" asked Mr. Robbins.

Sam, standing up again, said, "I object to this line of questioning and I demand that we stop until counsel is adequately prepared."

"Mr. Turner, as I indicated before, we need to expedite this hearing. You will have your turn to speak," Dr. Larson replied. "Please answer the question, Mrs. Allen."

Sam sat down. I could tell he was ready to explode. The interpreter was the only one at our table who seemed to be enjoying herself.

"Yes," Mrs. Allen answered. "I believe Juanita was in some sort of blind rage. She kept pushing Sheena's head down and I couldn't get her off. Mrs. Fellini had to help me."

"Thank you, Mrs. Allen. That will be all for tonight," Mr. Robbins told her. "Now I would like to get Mrs. Fellini's statement." The older white-haired lady sitting across from me, looked up.

"Please state your name," Mr. Robbins said.

"My name is Elizabeth Fellini. I work as as a teacher at Roosevelt High."

"Mrs. Fellini, can you tell us what you witnessed the day of the fight between Juanita Chávez and Sheena Martin?"

"Well, I really didn't see how the fight began. I was going through the building when I heard screams coming from the girls' locker room. So I went in there to see what was going on."

"What did you see when you went inside?"

"I saw all the girls in a circle. I pushed my way through and saw Janice struggling with Juanita to get her off of Sheena."

"Did Miss Martin appear to be injured?"

"Yes. She seemed dazed. She was lying on the floor."

"Would you say that Juanita Chávez was out of control?" asked Mr. Robbins.

"Well, I guess you could say that because I had to assist Janice in keeping her away from Sheena, who was struggling to get up."

"What happened next?"

"Once Juanita was calmed down, I took Sheena over to the school nurse's office. I believe Mrs. Allen took Juanita to the Dean of Students' office."

"Thank you, Mrs. Fellini. That is all for now. Dr. Larson, I have no further witnesses."

Dr. Larson thanked Mr. Robbins. Then he told Sam, "And now, Mr. Turner, we have about fifteen minutes left before we adjourn. You may present your case."

This time Sam did not bother standing up. "I am outraged by the school board's lack of courtesy. I cannot do justice to my client in fifteen minutes. I request a continuation and I demand that I be given as much time as I need at the next meeting to present my case—with my own witnesses, if necessary."

"Very well, Mr. Turner," Dr. Larson stated. "Unfortunately, we will not be able to meet until after the holidays. However, at that time, Mr. Turner, you will be given ample time to present your case. This meeting is adjourned."

Unlike the previous meetings, we didn't wait for the school board members to leave first. Sam immediately stood up and we all followed him out the door.

✎   ✐   ✐

That evening, I had trouble sleeping. I kept seeing Mr. Robbins' face leering at me across the room.

FIFTEEN
Ms. Martínez

The next morning , I woke up with a splitting headache. Frank scolded me and reminded me that I was overdoing it. I ignored his remarks, insisting that all I needed was a few more hours of sleep. After Frank left for work, I got out of bed, found my appointment book, and cancelled my two morning appointments. Then I climbed back into bed and tried to fall back asleep. It was useless. I kept going over last night's school board meeting in my head. It had been frightening. Even Sam had seemed intimidated. Juanita's scared face kept flashing in my mind. I wondered how she was feeling. It was a good thing I had scheduled an appointment with her this afternoon.

A half hour later, still unable to sleep, I was about to get out of bed when the phone rang. "Hello," I answered in a tired voice.

"Sandy, it's your mother."

"Oh, hello, Mom."

"I called your office and they said you were ill. Are you all right?" she asked.

"I'm fine, Mom. Just a little tired, that's all." It was just like my mother to worry about every little thing. She was probably already imagining that I had some sort of disease.

"Are you eating right? You looked so pale and skinny the last time you were here. I think you don't eat right."

I smiled to myself. My mother would think I was skinny even if I weighed 200 pounds. "I eat enough, Mom. How's Dad?"

"He's fine. I'm calling to find out if you are coming for Thanksgiving. You never called me back."

Frank was right. She never gave up. I might as well tell her now.

"Sorry, Mom. We're not going to make it. I'm so busy straight through to Thanksgiving, and I just don't feel up to a long drive." There, I had said it.

I could feel the silence at the other end of the line. Finally, my mother spoke up again. "If that's the way you feel, I guess you don't care to see us. I know you still blame us for Andy's death, don't you?"

My mother's voice was quivering as if she were about to cry. God, even after all these years, she still knew how to make me feel guilty. "That's not the way it is, Mom. You know I love you and Dad, but I just can't make it this year."

She was probably right. I did blame them. And I hated going back home to all that emptiness, the dull pain I felt every time I was there. Why couldn't she understand? I forced myself to continue.

"I just can't go this time, Mom. I'll call you back soon, okay? Now I need to get ready for my afternoon appointments. Talk to you later." The next thing I heard was a click at the other end of the line. Great. That was all I needed to round out my restful morning. I hung up the phone feeling worse than when I had awakened this morning.

When I arrived at my office, Juanita was sitting waiting for me in the reception area. I noticed that she was wearing a pink miniskirt with some white boots that reminded me of my old go-go boots from the sixties.

"Hello, Juanita. You look very pretty today," I told her.

"Thanks, Ms. Martínez," she answered very politely.

We walked back to my office and Juanita sat down across from me. She seemed quieter than usual, which was understandable after last night's board meeting.

"I'm sorry about the board meeting, Juanita. I know you must have felt very uncomfortable hearing your teachers talk about the fight. Sam and I had no idea that they were going to have witnesses. I'm really sorry."

"It's okay, Ms. Martínez. It's not your fault," Juanita said. "But I felt so ashamed hearing them say all those things. I wanted to crawl under the table. They made it sound like I'm a criminal or something. And they just blamed me for everything, not Sheena.

Juanita's eyes were filling with tears.

"I know they did, and they were wrong and unfair. Sometimes adults behave like children. You're not a criminal, and don't let anyone make you feel that way."

"Thanks, Ms. Martínez," Juanita said, wiping a tear from her face. I handed her a Kleenex.

"Sam and I thought you were very brave, Juanita. We're both very proud of you. And don't worry, Sam is an excellent attorney. He'll make sure they hear the entire story at the next board meeting."

"Do you think they'll bring Sheena to talk?" Juanita asked apprehensively.

"I'm not sure if they will. It would be better if they didn't. How do you feel about Sheena now?"

Juanita was silent for a few minutes. I knew that it was a difficult question to answer.

"I really don't know. I used to like her before. She was my friend at one time before she went out with Carlos. I even used to go to her house. I always felt sorry for her 'cause she didn't have a dad and her mom worked nights. So she was always alone after school."

"Do you know what her mother does?" I asked.

"I think she's a waitress and works nights, so Sheena's alone a lot. I used to kinda like her once."

Juanita's empathy for Sheena brought back memories of my childhood friend, Mary Wailes. She used to live in the same barrio as we did and she liked to hang out with all the Chicanos. Poor white trash, they used to say about her family. I had liked her a lot. Why was it that poor people seemed to suffer the most? I couldn't help but feel sorry for Sheena.

"What happened to end the friendship?" I asked Juanita.

"Well, she got mad 'cause Carlos didn't like her, and she just took it out on me and my family."

"Do you think you could get to like Sheena again if things were different?"

"I don't know. Sometimes I feel mad 'cause she's in school and I'm not. And she won't lay off of me. The other night at the Rock she was trying to pick on me."

"The Rock? What's that?" I asked, suddenly feeling anxious.

"You know, it's a dance club downtown, Rock and a Hard Place, but everyone calls it the Rock. I told you about teen night on Thursdays. Well, I went with Maya and Rina. Sheena was there and she got in my face really bad."

"What do you mean, she got in your face?" I asked.

"Well, Maya and I were coming out of the bathroom and Sheena was blocking my way and she started trying to pick a fight with me."

"What did you do then?"

"Well, I was getting really mad. I felt like popping her one. But I started thinking about what we talked about, how fighting is bad and how I should walk away. So I was getting ready to walk away when my brother got there and he took me home."

"Juanita, I'm really proud of you for not losing your temper. I know it's very difficult to control your anger in situations like that."

"Well, I really want to graduate, and I'm not going to let Sheena or anybody get me into a fight anymore."

"Do your parents know about all of this?" I asked, knowing what Juanita's answer would be.

"No. I feel bad 'cause I lied to them and said I was going to a game so I could go to the Rock. Carlos stuck up for me. He knew I lied, but he didn't tell my parents."

"It doesn't feel good to lie, does it, Juanita?"

"No. I was scared all night thinking my parents would find out. But Carlos didn't rat on me. I really hate lying, but it's the only way to get out of the house sometimes."

"Have you tried talking to your parents about dating?"

"*Híjole*, Ms. Martínez, my dad would pop me one if I mentioned it. He won't even let us talk to guys on the phone."

"Maybe your mom can help try to convince him."

"Yeah, I guess. I hope so 'cause I hate lying. But maybe next year he'll let me date, when I turn sixteen."

It was time to change the subject. "How is the tutoring coming along?"

Juanita's face lit up. "It's coming really good. I'm catching up with everything. It's a lot of work, but I don't want to get behind. I want to graduate with Maya and the guys."

"And you will graduate if you work hard. That's why it's important to keep up with your school work. Sam said we need to prove to the school board members that you're a good student. He also said we need to keep up our counselling sessions, at least once a month. Is that all right with you? You're not sick of me yet, are you?" I asked, smiling.

"No, I really like talking to you, Ms. Martínez. Maya was right. She said you were a nice person."

"Thank you very much, Juanita. I'm glad Maya thinks some shrinks are nice." We both laughed. "Now, if you don't mind, we'll stop because I have a very busy schedule this afternoon, since I only came in for half the day. I probably won't see you until sometime around December. I'll call you to set up the appointment."

"Okay, Ms. Martínez."

"Do you have a ride home?" I asked, standing up.

"Yeah. I just need to call my mom."

"Go ahead and use the telephone on the front desk," I said, walking Juanita to the door.

"Thanks, Ms. Martínez," Juanita said.

As I closed the door behind her, I noticed that my headache had disappeared and I was feeling much better.

SIXTEEN
Juanita

I don't know why Maya thinks I'm lucky. I get so sick and tired of cleaning the house and taking care of the three little ones. All they want to do is play. And Celia is such a pain. She follows me everywhere and snoops in my things. The other day I walked into the bedroom and caught her reading the letter Rudy wrote me. I grabbed it from her and she started teasing me, telling me she was going to tell 'Amá and 'Apá on me. I guess I need to hide Rudy's letters somewhere else.

I think Rudy really likes me. He keeps passing by our apartment with his friends. He pretends not to look this way, but I can tell he's hoping to see me. Maya says he keeps asking her when we're going to the Rock again. That would be so neat, but I hate sneaking out. I wish 'Apá would let me go out more. Why can't he be more like Maya's dad? He lets her go everywhere. And he already told her she can date when she turns sixteen. I don't know why 'Apá is so old-fashioned. It's not like we live in Mexico. All the girls in high school get to go out to dances except me, even fat Judy down the street. Maybe 'Amá can talk to 'Apá for me, like Ms. Martínez said. Maybe she can make him under-

stand. 'Amá always sticks up for me and Celia.

I really love my 'Amá. She never complains about anything, even when 'Apá goes drinking with his friends and doesn't come home until late. Sometimes 'Amá tells me about her life in Mexico when she was young, how she lived in a little town and slept in the same room with her ten brothers and sisters. 'Amá only went to third grade. She says that's the way it is in Mexico for poor people. 'Amá married my 'Apá when she was sixteen. She says she had no other choice. 'Amá says in Mexico that's the only thing girls did then: get married and have babies. That's why she says that I should study hard and not be a dummy. 'Amá wants me and Celia to graduate and be somebody like Ms. Martínez or Maya's mom.

SEVENTEEN
Juanita

A week later, Maya phones to invite me to eat at her house on Thanksgiving Day. She tells me that her parents are having a turkey dinner and she's allowed to invite her best friend. I ask my 'Apá and he gives me permission. We never celebrate Thanksgiving. 'Apá says he can't understand why people celebrate it. It's not a holiday in Mexico, so 'Apá doesn't understand it. Maya says she hates Thanksgiving. She says it's not true that the Pilgrims were so nice to the Indians. Maya has Navajo blood: that's why she's always sticking up for the Indians.

On Thursday, my parents drop me off at Maya's house on their way to San Martin. Maya lives in a mansion. Her house is about four times bigger than our apartment. I can't believe she has her own bedroom with a bathroom all to herself. She even has another room with a desk where she studies. She calls it her "thinking room." I think Maya's parents are rich.

Maya's mom is really nice. Her name is Sonia. She reminds me of Ms. Martínez 'cause she speaks both English and Spanish. I can see why Maya is so smart. Her mom is a professor and her dad is some sort of engineer. He speaks Spanish and English, too, and he's real tall and handsome. I guess that's why Maya is so tall.

At dinner, Maya's mom does most of the talking. She knows I'm from Mexico, so she tells me all about her trips to Mexico City and how much she loves speaking Spanish. Then she asks me how I like Ms. Martínez. She calls her "Sandy" like Sam does. She tells me that she had invited Ms. Martínez and her husband to dinner, but that Sandy wasn't feeling well. Maya pokes at her food. I guess that's why she's so skinny. Me, I'm a pig. I eat everything on my plate.

After dinner, we go to Maya's room. We put on the radio on and sit on the bed to talk.

"My mom gets on my nerves sometimes," Maya says. "She just talks and talks and my poor dad can't get a word in."

"She's really nice," I tell Maya. "And she's so pretty." I can't help but wish that my 'Amá looked like Maya's mom. Maya's parents are perfect. Her home is perfect, too.

"Yeah, I think she's pretty, too, but she sure gets on my nerves. Have you answered Rudy's letter yet?" Maya asks.

I reach for my purse and hand Maya the letter I wrote Rudy last night. "Would you give this to him?"

"*¡Híjole!* I think Rudy has a major crush on you."

"You really think so, Maya? I think Rudy's so cute. I just hope my brother doesn't find out we like each other. You know how he is."

"Don't be silly," Maya answers, stretching out her long brown legs across the bed. "Carlos doesn't hang out with him. Can you go to the mall with me on Saturday? Tyrone and the guys are supposed to be there. Rudy, too, I think."

"Really?" I ask Maya, feeling excited about the idea of seeing Rudy again. "I don't know if I can go. About what time are you going?"

"About one or two. I think my mom will give us a ride, but don't let Celia tag along, okay?"

"I'll try. But it depends on whether my 'Amá goes to work or not. If she does, then I have to baby-sit. And I don't know if they'll let me go without Celia. They always want me to drag her along everywhere I go even though I hate it."

"I know, but try to make it alone, okay? Let's do our nails. You do mine first and then I'll do yours. I just bought a new polish."

I watch Maya get up and walk over to the dresser for her manicure set. I am already wondering what I should wear on Saturday. Maybe I can borrow Celia's new skirt.

"Here," says Maya handing me the nail file and stretching out her hand to me. Even Maya's nails are perfect, long, and thick.

We spend the next hour doing our nails and listening to the radio. Then we turn the T.V. on and watch a movie on HBO. About 9:30, Maya's dad knocks on the door and tells me it's time to take me home.

✎   ✐   ✐

On Saturday, Maya's mother drops us off at the Town and Country Mall. I had to bribe Celia again so that she wouldn't tag along. I promised to wash the dishes for a whole week if she stayed home.

The mall is the local hangout. It's the only mall

in town, so everyone hangs out there. All the kids from the high school like to go there and just walk around the mall. Maya and I like to go to Macy's and get free make-overs. Then we try on all the samples of perfume. We like to try clothes on, too, but they're so expensive. Sometimes Maya has her mom's credit card and she buys something she likes. Maya is so lucky.

When we get bored at Macy's, we walk over to a bench and sit down to watch for cute guys. We are sitting down eating a Mrs. Fields' cookie when Tyrone, Tommy, and Rudy come up behind us.

"Hey, what's up?" Tyrone asks.

Maya gobbles down her last piece of cookie so that she can answer him. "Not much. What are you guys up to?"

"Just hanging out," Tyrone tells her.

Rudy is staring at me. This makes me so nervous that I can't finish my cookie. Tommy reaches over and grabs it out of my hand.

"Thanks, Johnny," he says.

Maya yells at him, "What a pig!"

"That's okay," I tell her, feeling my face changing colors.

Rudy is looking straight at me again. "Want to walk around with us?" he asks.

I manage to mumble "sure," trying hard not to look too excited. Maya, Tyrone, and Tommy have already started walking together. I notice that Tyrone is holding Maya's hand. Rudy and I follow behind.

"When do you think you'll be back in school?" Rudy asks.

"Soon, I hope. But I'm keeping up with my school work at home. I have a real nice tutor."

"That's good," Rudy says, suddenly getting quiet as we walk up the mall. I notice that people are staring at us. It's cause there aren't that many Mexicans and blacks in this town, so when we're all together, people stare more. Tyrone calls himself an African-American. Maya says it's to show you're proud of your African roots. She says it's like the word "Chicano," which shows you're proud of your Indian blood. I don't understand the word "Chicano," but it sounds neat.

After a few minutes, Rudy reaches for my hand. He squeezes it and I can feel my heart beating faster. I've never let a boy hold my hand before Rudy. We come to the snack bar and we decide to stop.

"Let's get a Coke," Maya says. Tyrone agrees. Maya is always like the leader of the group when we're together. Tommy goes along with whatever Tyrone says.

We get in line for a soda, and I let go of Rudy's hand so that I can get some money from my purse. My hand feels sweaty.

Afterwards, we go sit at a table. Maya sits between Tommy and Tyrone. Rudy is sitting next to me.

"Hey, Tommy. See that fat babe over there?" Tyrone says. "She's staring at you. I think she likes you." Tyrone likes to kid around a lot just like Tommy does.

"Which one? The one with all the zits? I think she likes you, Ty," Tommy tells him.

Everyone starts laughing. Tommy is so funny. He's real handsome, too. All the girls at school have a crush on him. Maya calls him a *güero* 'cause he's so light-complected.

We stay at the snack bar talking for about an

hour, making fun of all the people going by. Then the guys take off to play the video games. I think guys are so hyper; they always have to be doing something.

At five o'clock, Maya's mom picks us up in front of Macy's. She asks us if we had a fun time. Maya and I sneak a quick look at each other before we answer.

EIGHTEEN
Juanita

December is my favorite month of the year. I love to see the Christmas decorations downtown. The whole town is lit up with pretty lights. 'Apá likes to take us driving around the different neighborhoods at night so that we can see all the decorations people put up. 'Amá is always nervous at Christmas time 'cause we have hardly any money, and the three little ones want everything they see on the T.V. commercials.

My favorite part of Christmas is when we decorate our Christmas tree. Celia and I make popcorn so that we can string it on the tree. Even Carlos joins in. The three little ones try to help, but they end up eating more popcorn than they string. 'Amá taught us how to make *ojos de Dios* one year, so every Christmas we make new ones to put on our Christmas tree. They're so pretty and colorful. 'Amá says she used to make them in Mexico when she was a little girl. Her grandmother taught her how to make them.

On December 12, we all go to the special mass for the *Virgen de Guadalupe*. She's the patron saint of Mexico. This is the only time of the year that 'Apá actually goes to church with us. Every year on this night, everyone gathers outside the church and the priest leads a procession around the block and into the church. A group of *mariachis* go with us, and while they play, we sing songs for the Virgin. The altar boys carry a statue of Our Lady of Guadalupe.

The church is filled with Mexicans and with the red and green ribbons that symbolize the colors of the Mexican flag. A priest from San Martín always comes to give the mass in Spanish. All the Mexicans from the nearby towns come to this special mass. Every year, the priest tells the story of how the Virgin appeared in Mexico to a poor Indian named Juan Diego. Then some *señoras* go up to the altar and tell stories about how the Virgin has performed miracles for them. It's so beautiful, and it makes me feel really proud of being a Mexican.

Something else that I really like is that the week before Christmas, we drive to San Martin to my 'Apá's friends to celebrate *Las Posadas*. 'Amá says that *Las Posadas* are celebrated every year in Mexico. It's so much fun 'cause we get together with a group of friends and we go from house to house asking people if they have a *posada,* lodging, for us. The three little ones love *Las Posadas*. At each house we visit, we're invited in to drink Mexican hot chocolate and eat *pan dulce,* a big sweet roll. The little kids get candy, too. 'Amá says that *Las Posadas* are supposed to be like the night when Mary and Joseph were looking for a place to stay for the birth of baby Jesus. I used to get excited for *Las Posadas*, but now that I'm grown-up, I just like visiting with my friends. I wish we lived in San Martin.

On Christmas Eve, 'Amá always makes *ta-*

males. It is a day-long job. I love eating *tamales*, but it takes forever to make them. 'Amá prepares the corn dough, *masa,* and the meat filling. Then Celia and I help spread the *masa,* on the corn husks. Next, we put some of the meat with chile inside and roll the *tamal*. 'Amá taught us how to do this when we were real little. It looks easy, but it's kind of hard at first to learn to put the dough on the husks. This year we're trying to teach Rosario and Lupita, my two little sisters, how to do it. Markey is still too little.

By the evening, we're already steaming the *tamales*. 'Amá likes to make dozens and dozens 'cause she always gives some to all her friends and neighbors. Maya says my 'Amá's *tamales* are the best. Sometimes 'Apá invites his friends over and we have a big fiesta or *tamalada*.

We always open our presents on Christmas morning. The three little ones get to empty their socks first. Celia and I have stuffed them with candy. I don't know how 'Amá does it, but she always seems to get us each something we've been wanting. I get the new sweater I have been eyeing every time we go to J.C. Penney's, and Celia gets a Walkman. I hate those things. Carlos gets a new shirt and some shaving lotion. Celia and I tease him about it. 'Amá and 'Apá always give each other something. This year 'Apá gives 'Amá a new watch, and 'Apá gets new gloves. The little ones always get the most presents. 'Amá always buys them a bunch of small things. Then we spend the rest of the day eating *tamales*. We eat them for the next few days until we're sick of them.

Later that week, Maya phones to tell me that her mom said that Ms. Martínez is in the hospital.

I start to feel worried. I hope Ms. Martínez is okay. I don't know how I'll ever get back into school without her. I say a special prayer for her to the Virgin before I go to bed that night.

NINETEEN
Ms. Martínez

It seemed unbelievable that I was spending the Christmas holiday in the hospital with an IV hooked up to my arm. Damn it. I hated hospitals with a passion. Why did this have to happen to me now of all times? It must be *"la mala suerte,"* bad luck, as my grandmother used to say. I thought back to the events that had brought me here that horrible afternoon. I was sitting in my office getting ready for my next patient when I suddenly started to feel nauseated. I tried to get up, and before I knew it, I was vomiting. I managed to reach underneath my desk and pull out my wastebasket before I puked all over the carpet. After about a minute or two, the vomiting subsided and I leaned back in my chair, feeling terrible cramps in my abdomen. Then the vomiting started all over again. That was when I knew I was really sick.

I waited for the vomiting to stop and then dialed Frank's number at work. By then, the cramps had become more intense and I was beginning to feel weaker. When Frank arrived fifteen minutes later, he found me lying down on the couch holding my hand tightly over my stomach. Frank helped me out to the car and drove me straight to the doctor's office.

After he had examined me, the doctor explained that I had some sort of virus and that I needed to be hospitalized. I tried to talk him out of it, promising to go home and spend the entire day in bed. But it was useless. The next thing I knew, Frank was having me admitted into the hospital. And now, here I was in bed feeling miserable at Christmas time.

I really disliked being in the hospital. It was almost impossible to get any sleep because the nurses keep coming in every two hours to check my IV. And the woman next to me snored all night. I was hoping that the doctor would let me go home as soon as possible. My patients needed me. Frank needed me. Poor Frank. All I'd done for the past two days was complain about having to be stuck here during the holiday. Frank didn't get upset. He listened to me patiently. I don't know what I'd do without him.

The sound of footsteps interrupted my thoughts, and I turned to look at the doorway. Oh, God, it was my mother.

"Sandy, I came as soon as Frank told me," she said, pulling up a chair next to the bed so that she could be closer to me.

I tried not to appear upset at her unexpected appearance. "Mom, what are you doing here? It's so far for you to come. When did you get here?"

"I got here late last night. I thought you might need some help until you get back on your feet again. Your dad didn't want to come. You know how he hates traveling. And we both hated for you to be alone at Christmas."

"I'm not alone, Mom. Frank is with me," I told

her, trying hard to conceal my frustration.

"Yes, I know, *m'ija*, but Frank works all day and I know he can't take too many days off, so I've come to stay with you until you feel better."

I could hear the concern in her voice. I knew she meant well. After all, wasn't that how mothers were supposed to behave? A few days couldn't hurt. I tried to sound cheerful. "That's nice of you, Mom. The doctor said I can go home in a few days if my fever is completely gone."

"I knew you were working too hard, Sandy, especially when you didn't come for Thanksgiving."

It was unbelievable, but my mother always seemed to know how to make me feel guilty. She treated me more like a teenager than like an adult. I debated how to respond. It was hopeless; she always won. Why argue with her?

"Mom, I'm feeling a little sleepy," I said, faking a yawn and hoping that she would take the hint.

"You go right ahead and sleep, *m'ija*. I brought a magazine to read," she said, reaching for her handbag.

Oh, well, as Frank would say, "If you can't beat them, join them. "I turned over on my side and pretended to go to sleep.

✎ ✐ ✐

Two days later, I was back home feeling like a prisoner again. Or maybe a baby. I wasn't sure which one. My mother insisted that I stay in bed until ten or eleven every day, even though I kept telling her that I was feeling fine again. She was driving me crazy. She'd already rearranged the entire living room, reorganized the kitchen cupboards, and she kept cooking huge dinners. I knew that she was hoping to fatten me up. Frank loved it, though. He kept right on eating everything my mother made in spite of the fact that I told him he was going to get fat. He ignored me, telling me to relax and reminding me that my mother was only here for a week. A week to me seemed like an eternity.

One evening during dinner, I couldn't take it any more and I snapped at her. Frank apologized quickly for my rudeness, but not before I saw my mother's eyes fill with tears. Later that night, I had trouble sleeping because I felt so guilty for snapping at her.

Frank was probably right. I was too hard on my mother. But I couldn't stand her over-protectiveness. That's exactly how she had been with Andy all those years. Maybe if she hadn't been that way, he'd still be alive. Oh, God, my mother was right. I did blame them for Andy's death. But maybe I was to blame just as much as they were. Maybe if I'd been with him that night I could have stopped him. I should never have left him behind and gone away. I should have gone back for him. If anyone had known how hard it was living at home, it had been me—seeing dad drunk all the time, the constant arguments. All that pain. The last time I had been home, Andy had seemed quieter than usual. I remember teasing him about girls at dinner time. Then we had watched T.V. together. When I invited him to go see a movie with me, he had begged off, saying he was busy with the guys. He left in mom's car. When I told mom that I thought Andy was too young to be driving her car, she had defended him, telling me he was very responsible. She always spoiled him.

The police report said Andy was high on alcohol and cocaine the night he died. It also stated that it appeared to be a suicide, since they couldn't find any skid marks. His car had crashed straight into an electric pole. I went back home that night. Mom was hysterical and dad was sober for a change. At the funeral, I swore I'd never go home again.

I fell asleep remembering Andy's funeral and my mother's sobs. I promised myself that I would try to be more patient with my mother.

TWENTY
Ms. Martínez

Several weeks later I was back at work, amazed that I had survived both the hospital stay and my mother's visit. My mother had finally decided to go back home once the doctor gave me a clean bill of health. At the bus station, I had thanked her, promising that I wouldn't work so hard.

My first week back at the office seemed to go by quickly, and before I knew it, it was time to get ready for my next appointment with Juanita. It had been over a month since I had last seen her. I hoped that her holidays had been better than mine.

Feeling excited about my meeting with Juanita, I hurried out to the reception area at exactly four o'clock. I found Juanita sitting down reading a teen magazine.

"Hello, Juanita. How are you?" I asked.

Juanita put her magazine down and stood up to greet me. "Hi, Ms. Martínez. I'm fine, but how about you? Maya told me you were sick and in the hospital."

I walked up to her and gave her a big hug. "Don't worry about me. You know what they say about good old Mexican blood. It's stronger than ever."

Juanita smiled and followed me back to my

office. We sat down in our usual places. I noticed that Juanita was carrying a brown paper bag.

"I brought you this, Ms. Martínez," she said, handing me the bag.

"Oh, thank you, Juanita. Something sure smells good," I told her, opening the bag to look inside.

"They're some *tamales* my mom sent you. We made them for Christmas and we froze some for New Year's."

"God, I love *tamales*, so does Frank. We'll have these for dinner," I said, putting the bag on my desk. "Did you help make them?"

"Yeah, my sister and I always help my mom, but we're sick of them now."

I smiled. "I know the feeling. When my mother used to make them, that's all we ate for weeks."

"Maya said you went to her house on New Year's Eve?" Juanita asked.

"Oh, yes. You see, Sonia and I are old friends, so once in a while we get together. We had a good time."

Juanita's face lit up. "There's an old Mexican saying that what you do on New Year's Eve is what you'll be doing the rest of the new year. My mom told me that."

"Really? Well, that's nice. I guess I'll be visiting with friends a lot this year." I waited for Juanita to speak. She seemed eager to lead the conversation this afternoon.

After about a minute, Juanita said, "I think Maya's family is perfect."

I laughed out loud. "Don't be silly, Juanita. Nobody has a perfect life. It might look perfect, but there's no such thing. Everyone has problems. Now tell me, how are you? It's been a whole month since I last saw you."

"I guess I'm doing real good. I'm keeping up with all my school work. My tutor is real nice."

"That's great, Juanita. Sam will be pleased. He said the school board would be impressed if you kept up with all your classes. You do remember that the next school board meeting is at the end of this month, right?"

Juanita's smile disappeared. She hesitated before answering, "Yeah, I know. I guess I'm starting to feel really nervous about it."

I watched as Juanita reached for a strand of hair and began twirling it.

"Don't worry, Juanita. I'll be right there next to you. I know that this meeting will be extra stressful for you because Sam will be presenting your case. But it's important that you're there so that they can see how much you really care about going back to school."

"Yeah, I know," Juanita said, letting go of the strand of hair. "I'll try not to be so nervous."

"How are things at home?"

"I guess everything is good. I have a boyfriend." Juanita's face was turning red.

"Really?" I asked. "Who is he?"

"His name is Rudy. He's a sophomore at Roosevelt like me, and he lives over where I do."

"What is Rudy like?"

Juanita smiled. "He's really cute. He's nice, too."

"You said your dad won't let you date. So how do you get to see him? Does he call you?" I asked, thinking back to my first boyfriend. I was in ninth grade and his name was Dan Wailes, the only *gringo* who hung out with the Chicanos. I had a bad crush on him and I used to sneak out from the football games to be with him. Juanita's voice pulled me back from the past.

"No, Rudy can't call me on the phone. But we write to each other," Juanita answered. "Maya brings me his letters. Sometimes Tommy does, too."

"Who is Tommy?" I asked.

"Oh, he's a good friend. He lives next door to me, and we walk to school together sometimes."

"I guess it's exciting to have a boyfriend, right?"

"Yeah. Kinda. Except I get nervous around him. I was walking with him at the mall and Maya was with Tyrone, this guy she likes, and well, we were holding hands, and I got really nervous. Maya says that's silly of me, that a lot of the girls are already making out with guys. But I haven't yet. Maya even said this one girl at Roosevelt is pregnant and she's only sixteen."

I knew that I had to be careful on how I phrased my next question. "Have they had any classes on sex education at the high school yet?"

Juanita was looking down at her skirt. I could tell that she was embarrassed. "Yeah, my freshman year in P.E., they told us all about it. I'm still a virgin and I'm staying like that until I get married, even if people spread lies like Sheena did." Juanita was looking at me now.

"Good for you, Juanita," I said. "I know that peer pressure is really difficult for teenagers today. And there are so many teen pregnancies today."

"Yeah, I know, Ms. Martínez. And it's scary about AIDS, too."

"That's why it's so important to have sex education." I was feeling braver now that she was opening up on such a difficult subject. "Do they have condom machines at your school?"

"I don't know. They were talking about it last year," Juanita said, pulling at her skirt.

I knew that it was time to stop. It was always difficult for teenagers to talk about sex. "We should stop for today, Juanita. Do you need a ride home? You're my last appointment."

Juanita seemed relieved. "Sure, Ms. Martínez. If it isn't much trouble."

"Of course not," I said.

✎   ▭   ✐

When I dropped Juanita off at her apartment, I couldn't help but notice the neighborhood she lived in—typical low-income housing, concrete playground, no room to breathe. I knew the feeling only too well. It was tough for the kids here, just as it had been for me all those years.

TWENTY-ONE
Ms. Martínez

I squeezed Juanita's hand as we waited for Dr. Larson to give his opening remarks to the board members. I hadn't slept all night in anticipation of tonight's events. The last board meeting had been a nightmare. But I was certain that Sam would knock them off their seats tonight.

Dr. Larson leaned into the microphone and began speaking. "Let me remind all of you that this is a closed session to discuss the Juanita Chávez case. Tonight Mr. Sam Turner, counsel for the defendant, will give his presentation to the board members. We have agreed to give Mr. Turner as much time as he needs this evening. If necessary, we will take a short recess at some point. Please reserve your comments or questions until he has concluded. You may begin, Mr. Turner."

Unlike me, Sam did not appear to be nervous. Very calmly, he cleared his throat and began speaking. "Thank you, Dr. Larson. I have prepared a declaration for Miss Chávez after extensive interviews, and I am convinced of her honesty and sincerity. Before I pass out copies of Juanita's declaration for the board members to read, I would like to express some concerns I have on behalf of Miss

Chávez.

"First, I was made to understand by the school administration that these hearings would be informal, a sort of sitting around the table to discuss the case. I had indicated that I too preferred a non-confrontational setting. Then at the last hearing, when the school attorney began to interrogate the Dean of Students, I realized that the hearing had turned formal instead of informal. This change came to my attention only after you started. I should have been notified of this change in procedure in advance.

"Second, I was also told that the family had a complete set of documents on this case. However, at the last meeting, when the school attorney began handing out a package to the board members, I was taken aback that the Chávez family did not have a copy of that document from which your attorney began to interrogate Mr. Jones and the two other surprise witnesses. If the board can receive dressed-up and complete documentation, so can the parents—out of respect, and in the spirit of fairness. There was some discussion at the last meeting that I should have asked for the document you presented. However, one cannot ask for what one does not know exists. I view it insulting to the parents that they were not presented a package of materials for the defense of their daughter that was as complete and well prepared as what the board received.

"Third, just before the beginning of the hearing I was handed the decision, or proposed decision, of the board regarding the expulsion. This document seems to me to eliminate the need for a hearing, since the decision has already been made without hearing the views of Miss Chávez or her family, not to mention her counsel. As a matter of fact, I was astounded at the decision and the procedural methods used to reach it and to announce it. It reminds me of Alice in Wonderland, where the White Queen said, 'No! No! Sentence first, then the verdict.' The board should have been required to look at the conduct of both parties and the circumstances that led to the incident. Had that been done, Sheena Martin very likely would have been found to have had a history of confrontational incidents, including racial remarks aimed at the Chávez family and other ethnic groups.

"Lastly, you could see and hear from the discourteous way I was treated by the board members at the last hearing that grace, courtesy, and politeness were in short supply. This was very frightening to the mother, daughter, and to Dr. Martínez. Mr. Chávez was disgusted and angry. He was surprised at the rudeness of educated people."

There was a brief pause as Sam reached for a glass of water. I noticed that the board members were all silent, perhaps shocked by Sam's defense.

Sam was indeed a brilliant speaker. I felt I was back in the '60s, taking part in a protest march. Even Juanita seemed to be hanging on every word Sam spoke. She was wide-eyed and alert. Good. This was a great learning experience for her.

Sam stood up and began circulating copies of Juanita's declaration. "Now, Dr. Larson, before I continue, I would like to ask for a brief recess so that the board members can read the declaration I have prepared for my client."

Dr. Larson consented. The room filled with silence as the board members proceeded to read

Juanita's declaration. I reached over and patted Sam on the hand. "Bravo, Sam."

He smiled at me and whispered, "I've only just begun. Notice how uncomfortable they're beginning to feel?"

Then Sam looked at Juanita. "How are you doing, young lady?"

Juanita smiled shyly. "I'm doing good, thank you."

"Good. Just make sure you don't fall asleep," Sam told her jokingly.

Twenty minutes later, Dr. Larson stated that the board members were ready for Sam to proceed with his defense. Sam leaned forward, eager to begin speaking. "In referring to my client's declaration, I would like for everyone to note the racial insults to the Chávez family, the privacy violations, and the disclosure of my client's academic standing by Sheena Martin to other students as well as to Miss Chávez without her permission. Notwithstanding our claim regarding due process and equal treatment, please do not misunderstand the position the family is taking. They are not saying that Juanita Chávez was right, or that her conduct should be condoned. They are saying that if Juanita Chávez is to be expelled, with charges filed against her and no evidence taken before the expulsion, then Sheena Martin should get the same treatment. They are saying that if a white student can start a fight and be repulsed by a Mexican-American student who in the school official's words 'put up a good fight,' then the actions of the Mexican-American student in defending herself cannot be the basis for disciplinary action which exceeds what was meted out to the white student; that the punishment in fact, should not be as great. They are also saying that there is a need to take in to account uncharged confrontations which the white student has been party to, especially when racial attacks and slurs have occurred.

"As it stands, there is a strong perception in the Latino community that Roosevelt High School, among other institutions, is racist toward Mexican-Americans. I am in a position having spent enough time with some members of that group to know that this perception is strong in this community. While this is not an excuse for whatever Miss Chávez did, it should be kept in mind that it takes two to tango. According to my witnesses, Miss Martin, a young white woman, made the first physical contact by shoving Miss Chávez very hard in the chest and then pulling her down as they struggled. Miss Martin struck her head on the bench. The parties had to be separated. Miss Martin is back in school. Miss Chávez is not in school. It would seem to me that treatment by the school district of these two young women was not equal.

"I have for many years worked in civil rights and employment discrimination. From my own experience, it is my opinion that the women were not treated equally. I also want to point out to you the romantic relationship that existed between Miss Martin and Miss Chávez's brother; that he rejected her for remarks she made about his family, and that she threatened to 'get even' with Miss Chávez. Please note the use of the words 'bitch' and 'ho.' These words, to me, don't mean much, but my witnesses have indicated that among women of the Mexican-American culture, there are few words which excite more passion. Miss Martin's getting into the school records and broadcasting disparaging information to the other students also was highly embarrassing to Miss Chávez. Miss Chávez did not use such tactics against Miss Martin and had no access to records. Overlooked in this whole equation is how reactions to Miss Martin's behavior were different depending on the cultural background of those who judged it. You are no doubt aware of Miss Martin's comments on blacks, which were voiced at a time when Miss Chávez's brother was considering dating a young Puerto Rican woman. It would be difficult for Miss Martin to make a case for not being prejudiced.

"I want to point out, too, that the level of assistance provided the Chávez family by the board appears to be much less than what was given Sheena Martin. For instance, the school directly assisted Sheena Martin in filing an assault and battery complaint against Juanita Chávez. The school district did not assist Juanita Chávez in filing an action against Sheena Martin, who actually was the one to make the first physical contact. From all the testimony, it appears that finger was pointed at Juanita Chávez while Sheena Martin was viewed as being relatively innocent. Yet, from the statements of the witnesses I interviewed, Sheena Martin struck the first blow. It was a hard shove. I asked Juanita to shove me the way she was shoved by Sheena, and if anyone had shoved me that hard, I also would have responded physically. Furthermore, Mrs. Chávez indicated that one of the school officials told her after the incident by telephone that Juanita had 'put up a good fight,' and laughed. I have not seen nor heard any evidence that the Chávez family was counselled to file charges against Sheena Martin.

"I would like to resolve this matter expeditiously, without the necessity of going to court. However, if my client desires to pursue the matter, I can tell you that I believe this case would do well in court. It appears to have wide implications for the school system also. The school system does not have a very reassuring local reputation for racial fairness, and this needs to be addressed. It is my opinion, that given Sheena's conduct before the fight, the suspensions of both students should have been equal, and had all the facts been considered, they would have been. In fact, the racial slurs by Sheena Martin would or should have resulted in her expulsion a long time ago, after adequate warnings, of course."

In looking at the possibility of a trial, your clients should consider the effectiveness of my client as a witness. Miss Chávez is polite, well-dressed, and makes a good appearance. She is a young woman of considerable charm. There are no signs of drugs or 'hardness.' She has not indulged in vandalism, graffiti, or other conduct which would make a bad student. She performs well in school. Her tutoring is successful. She is doing well in counselling. And she comes from a large family struggling to find the American Dream. Her parents are the salt of the earth. I do not wish to bring in student witnesses, but if necessary I will. Also, if the board believes that the Chávez family lacks the funds to pursue justice, I should advise you that the minority community is ready to assist them. Thank you, Dr. Larson. That is all I have to say."

I looked around the room. The board members were speechless, except for the school board attor-

ney who was talking in a low voice with Dr. Larson.
I whispered to Sam, "I think you've intimidated
them."

Sam smiled. "That was my intention."

I turned to Juanita and said, "Wasn't Sam brilliant?" Juanita nodded very calmly, as if she were
beginning to feel sure of herself again. Then I told
Mr. and Mrs. Chávez that Sam had done an out-
standing job and that they had nothing to worry
about. They also seemed reassured by Sam's performance this evening.

After a few minutes, Dr. Larson spoke for the
last time. "Thank you, Mr. Turner. We're out of
time. That concludes our hearing for this evening.
Our attorney will be in touch."

Sam thanked him again and then instructed
us to remain seated. Feeling triumphant, we
watched quietly as the board members filed out of
the room, talking in hushed voices to each other.

TWENTY-TWO
Juanita

February is the most boring month of the year. Nothing exciting ever happens in February. And now that I'm home all the time, it's even more boring. The little ones can be such a pain. Today 'Amá has gone to work with 'Apá in the fields so I have to take care of them by myself. At least Rosario and Lupita are out of my hair until two o'clock. But as soon as they get home, Lupita starts picking on Markey. She's so jealous of Markey, and Markey is so spoiled it makes her madder. I can't wait 'til Celia gets home from school so that I can dump them off on her for a while.

I wish I could go to school again. Ms. Martínez thinks I'll be back by spring break. She says Sam really scared them at the last school board meeting. I hope so, 'cause they sure scare me when I'm there. I feel like crawling under the table. I sure hope Sheena doesn't have to testify. I'll feel so embarrassed if she does. I won't know how to act. I can hardly wait until all of this is over. I want to go back to Roosevelt so bad that it hurts inside. Sometimes at night when everyone is asleep, I cry 'cause I miss school so much.

✎ ✏ ✐

On Saturday, Maya phones to tell me that there is a Sweetheart Dance at school next week for Valentine's Day. She says that Rudy and Tyrone are both going to be there, and she is wondering if I can go with her. She begs me to ask for permission to go with her and Rina.

That evening, I'm feeling real brave so I decide to ask my 'Apá. He's always in a better mood on Saturdays. Everyone is in the living room watching *Sábado Gigante*. I just can't stand Don Francisco on that show. And the audience is just as stupid, standing up and singing to all the commercials. I want to throw up every time they do that.

I sit down on the floor next to Markey. Carlos is not home, so it's a good time to ask 'Apá. Using my best Spanish, I explain to 'Apá that there is a dance next Friday to celebrate Valentine's Day. I tell him that Maya has invited me to go with her. 'Apá turns to look at me. Before he can say anything, I tell him that it is from seven to ten and that Maya's dad will pick me up and bring me home.

I can feel my heart beating faster. Celia and 'Amá are both looking at me. 'Apá tells me that I can't go, that I'm not old enough yet to be going to dances without my parents. I know that I shouldn't argue with him, but I feel so angry. I remind him that I'm almost sixteen, that I'm not a baby. But this is useless. 'Apá has already turned away to watch Don Francisco. I can feel my eyes start to get watery. I notice 'Amá's look of pity. For once, Celia doesn't say anything mean. I get up to leave the room.

As I'm climbing the stairs, I can hear 'Amá telling 'Apá that I'm more grown up than he thinks, that I am not a baby anymore, and that he can't keep me locked up forever. 'Apá tells her to shut up. Back in my room, I let myself fall face down on the bed and I start to cry. Sometimes I hate 'Apá. He makes me so mad. It's not fair, the way he is. Why is he so strict? Why can't he be like Maya's dad? I hate him. I wish I were dead. Sometimes I hate my whole life. I cry myself to sleep.

✑   ✐   ✎

Later that evening, I hear loud voices. I get out of bed and tiptoe to the edge of the stairs. 'Apá and Carlos are arguing. I sit on the top step to listen. 'Apá is angry cause Carlos wants to quit school and go to work. 'Apá tells him that he can't quit school, that he doesn't want him to have to work in the fields all day like he does. But Carlos keeps insisting that he's going to quit. 'Apá finally orders Carlos to shut up and go to bed.

Before I have time to sneak back into my room, Carlos is standing behind me. He doesn't look very happy.

"Aren't you in bed yet?" he asks me.

"I had to make *pipí*," I lie.

"*¡Chismosa!* I bet you heard everything, didn't you?"

"I couldn't help it. You were both shouting. Carlos, why do you want to be stupid and drop out of school?"

"I don't know. I guess I'm just tired of being poor. I want to work, have some money to myself so I can go out, get a car like the other guys."

"Don't be stupid, Carlos. It's better to finish

school," I tell him in a scolding tone.

"How would you know, you're just a dumb girl. It's late. Go to bed," Carlos orders me, walking towards his room.

I climb back in bed, hoping that Celia doesn't wake up. I can't sleep. I lie awake for a long time thinking about Carlos. 'Apá is right. He can't quit school. I know 'Apá won't let him do it. I guess 'Apá isn't so bad after all. He wants us all to be smart so we don't have to work hard like him. I guess he can't help that he's so strict. Maybe next year, when I turn sixteen, he'll let me go to the school dances. I fall asleep feeling hopeful, wishing I were a boy like Carlos so that I could go wherever I wanted.

TWENTY-THREE
Juanita

A few days after the Sweetheart Dance, I'm sitting in the living room watching cartoons with the little ones when someone knocks. Celia gets up and opens the door.

It's Maya. "Hi Celia, is anyone home?"

Celia invites her in right away. She loves it when Maya comes over 'cause she gets to snoop and listen to us talk about boys. Maya spots me sitting on the couch. "Hey, Johnny. Are you watching the Ninja Turtles? Hi, Rosie. Hi, Lupita," Maya says, walking over to where Markey is sitting and ruffling his hair.

The little ones really like it when Maya visits 'cause sometimes she sits down and plays with them. I think Maya's crazy. I decide to grab her before she has time to sit down and play with Markey.

"Hi, Maya. Want to go to my room?" I ask .

"Sure. Bye, Markey. See you later, alligator," Maya says with a smile.

I turn to Celia and warn her, "It's your turn to watch them 'til 'Amá gets home." Celia glares at me.

"Where's your mom?" Maya asks as we go upstairs.

"She went to work with my 'Apá and they don't get home 'til real late. Celia and I are supposed to take turns watching them. Carlos is lucky; he's never here."

Inside my room, Maya kicks off her shoes and sits cross-legged on my bed.

"Sorry, your dad didn't let you go to the dance with us. It wasn't that much fun without you. Rudy was there. He asked for you, and guess what? He sent you something."

Maya reaches inside her purse and pulls out a red envelope. "Rudy said to give this to you when I saw you," she says, handing me the envelope.

"He sent me this?" I ask Maya, feeling my heart beat faster. I decide to go ahead and open it in front of Maya. After all, she is my best friend.

It's a beautiful valentine with two hearts hooked together by Cupid. Rudy has written my name in one heart and his in the other one.

"I told you he had a crush on you," says Maya. "What did he write on it?"

I show it to Maya.

"*¡Híjole!* That guy is hot for you," she says, reading out loud. "With love, Rudy."

My face is turning red so I get up and go over to my dresser. I open my bottom drawer and hide my valentine under a bunch of clothes where Celia can't possibly find it.

"Did Tyrone give you one, too?" I ask Maya, sitting back down on the bed.

"Are you kidding? He gave me this giant box of candy."

"Was the dance fun?"

"Yeah. I guess," Maya answers. "But it was sort of dead without you. Rina and Ankiza went with me. We danced to every single dance. I think Rina likes Tyrone. She kept trying to flirt with him."

"Did Tyrone know she was flirting with him?"

"Yeah. He said she does it a lot when I'm not around, but he just ignores her."

"Was Sheena there?" I ask Maya, remembering when I saw her at the Rock.

"Yeah. But we just ignored her. She was with this other girl who has a bad rep. We all sort of feel sorry for her. She doesn't have any friends. No one at school likes her because she lies so much."

"Yeah. I know, like she lied about me. I don't hate her or anything either."

Maya stretches out her long brown legs across the bed. "The music was cool. They played Rap music all night. Ty and I were hot. I learned this new step. Watch," Maya says, standing up. "Turn your radio on and I'll show you."

I reach over to my tape deck and put on one of my tapes. Maya starts dancing. I watch closely as she tries to show me the steps to the new dance. Maya is so good at everything. I wish I were more like her. If only I were tall and thin and not such a *chaparra*.

After a few minutes, Maya sits down again. "Listen, do you think you can go to the mall with me on Saturday? Tyrone and Rudy want to meet us there. My mom can drop us off," Maya asks.

"On Saturday? I guess I can if 'Amá doesn't go work with 'Apá." My mind races ahead to Saturday. I'm already wondering what I will wear.

"Good. I'll tell the guys that we'll meet them. Maybe we can get there by noon."

"Okay. But I have to check with 'Amá first to

see if she's working or not."

"That's cool. I'll call you on Friday. Oh, my mom talked to Ms. Martínez the other night, and Ms. Martínez told her she thinks you'll be back in school soon. Is that true?"

"Yeah. Both Sam and Ms. Martínez think maybe they'll let me go back after spring break."

"That would be so neat. I sure hope so. It's a bummer at lunch time without you. Ankiza yaks all the time and Rina gets on everyone's nerves. She's always trying to flirt with Tyrone."

"Does she flirt with Rudy, too?" I blurt out.

Maya laughs. "Don't be an idiot!" she says. "She only likes Tyrone."

I start to laugh and before I know it, Maya and I are having a laugh attack.

TWENTY-FOUR
Juanita

On Saturday, Maya's mother drops us off at the mall. She reminds us that she'll come by and pick us up in front of Macy's at three. I'm so excited about seeing Rudy again, but at the same time I feel nervous about not telling my parents that we're meeting boys.

I decide to wear the new red sweater that 'Amá gave me for Christmas. Everyone always tells me how good red looks on me with my dark skin. I had to bribe Celia again so that she would lend me her blue-jean skirt. I promised I'd let her listen to all my Rap tapes.

"Where are we supposed to meet them?" I ask Maya as we walk through Macy's.

"They said they'd be over by the snack bar."

We're at the center of the mall when Maya suddenly stops at a boutique to look at the outfits hanging on the clothes rack at the front of the store. She pulls a black bra-like top from the rack and holds it up to her. "Now, if I only had your boobs, Johnny, then I could wear this."

I laugh and tell her, "Don't be such a pig, Maya!"

We continue walking through the mall when Maya stops again. This time it's at a jewelry boutique. She holds up a pair of earrings. "Did I tell you that Rina wants to pierce her nose? She wants me to do it, too. But my mom said I was crazy and she'd let me do it over her dead body."

"I think that's gross, piercing your nose," I tell her. "I wouldn't do it."

"It's the latest thing, Juanita. No more ear piercing. Now it's noses."

We start to laugh again. Some people stare at us. I guess they think we're crazy.

As we get close to the snack bar, Maya spots Tyrone and Rudy. They're standing next to Mrs. Fields' Cookies.

"Hey," Maya yells at them.

They start walking toward us. Rudy looks at me and smiles.

"Hi, Johnny."

I can feel my heart doing weird things again. "Hi, Rudy," I answer, noticing that he's wearing a Laker tee-shirt.

Maya walks up to Tyrone and gives him a playful punch on the shoulder. "Hey, what's happening?"

"Just waiting for you guys. What took you so long?" Tyrone asks, returning the punch.

"Not much. We just stopped to look in a few places."

"Yeah. I bet. I know girls. Listen, how about we walk to the park over by the lake across from the mall?"

Maya turns to look at me. I can tell she's up for it. "You want to, Johnny?" she asks me.

I know that it won't do me any good to say no. Maya always gets her way. I guess that's why she's the leader and I'm not. Rudy and Tyrone are both looking at me, waiting for my answer. "Sure," I answer.

We turn and walk out the side entrance and head for the park. I'm feeling nervous. My head is spinning with weird thoughts. I have never been to a park with a boy before. If 'Apá knew, he'd kill me. I sure hope Carlos doesn't happen to drive by with his friends and see me. I'm so nervous that I almost cross the street on the red light. But Rudy grabs me by the hand and stops me.

"Hey! Don't get run over, okay?" Rudy tells me.

I mumble something to him, hoping that he doesn't let go of me. I let him hold my hand the rest of the way. Maya and Tyrone walk ahead of us. When we get to the park, they take off toward the swings. Rudy and I sit on the first bench we see.

"Too bad you couldn't make it to the dance," Rudy says.

"Yeah, I know. I really wanted to go. Thanks for the Valentine. I really liked it."

"That's good. I sure hope you get back to school soon."

I can tell that Rudy is embarrassed. I thought only girls got embarrassed. I glance towards the swings. Tyrone has his arms around Maya, and I think he's kissing her. Embarrassed, I look away.

"I wanted to ask you something, Johnny," Rudy tells me, avoiding my eyes.

"Yeah, what?"

Rudy is finally looking at me. "Will you go steady with me?"

I can feel my face burning. I'm so excited. I've never gone steady before.

"Well, what do you say?" Rudy asks.

"Yeah, sure," I tell him.

Rudy reaches into his pocket, takes out a ring,

and before I know it, he slips it onto my right hand. "It's a little big for you, but maybe you can fix it."

Rudy puts his arm around me and leans forward to kiss me. I close my eyes and I can feel his lips on me. I smell his after-shave as he kisses me. I'm glad when he stops kissing me, 'cause I'm beginning to feel very warm all over. I've never felt this way before. It scares me.

We sit quietly, holding hands, watching the birds circling over the mountains. This is the most exciting day of my life.

After a short while, Maya and Tyrone walk over to where we're sitting. We all decide to climb the mountain for the fun of it. When we get to the top, we sit and talk for a few minutes. From up here, we can see the entire mall. We rest for about fifteen minutes and then decide to head back down.

On the way back to the mall, Rudy holds my hand. Maya and I share secret looks with each other. We wish this afternoon would never end.

Later that evening, I'm sitting in my room daydreaming about Rudy. I look at the ring he has given me and I feel warm all over again. I decide to put it on a chain so that I can wear it around my neck. This way I can put it inside my blouse and hide it. Not even Celia with her big mouth can see it. I can hardly wait to see Ms. Martínez so that I can tell her all about it.

TWENTY-FIVE
Ms. Martínez

It had been another one of those long, stressful mornings. My head was aching and I felt depressed. Rain always depressed me. Of course, having Beth completely fall apart in our morning appointment hadn't helped much. It had taken almost half an hour to calm her down. Poor Beth. She just couldn't accept the fact that her husband was gone, and she needed to replace her old life with a new one.

The afternoon had been almost as tiring. I had forced myself to skip lunch in order to catch up on my paperwork. Then it seemed like I was bombarded with one patient after another until I felt my head was going to burst. By four o'clock, I felt completely wasted. I couldn't even bear to think about what I would cook for dinner, nor about returning Sonia's phone call. It seemed odd that Sonia had called me at work. Come to think of it, the last time we had talked, she had seemed a bit on edge. Maybe Maya was giving her some problems. Could it be that Maya wasn't as perfect as Juanita seemed to think?

I looked at my watch. It was time for Juanita's appointment. I hadn't talked with her since the last board meeting. Since then, I had been feeling more optimistic, hoping that Sam had intimidated the school administration so that they would rescind their decision. Juanita deserved another chance. It was difficult enough being a teenager these days.

When I stepped into the reception area, Juanita was there waiting for me. She was holding a brown paper bag.

"Hello, Juanita. I'm sure glad to see you today."

She smiled. "Here, Ms. Martínez. My dad sent you these."

I reached for the bag, looking inside. "Yummy, I love strawberries. So does Frank."

"My dad picked them himself. It's the picking season now."

"That was very nice of him. Tell him thank you. Okay, young lady, follow me." Juanita followed me to my office, and the minute we sat down, she started to speak.

"Guess what, Ms. Martínez? Remember I told you about Rudy? Well, he asked me to go steady a few weeks ago."

Juanita's eyes were shining and her face had a glow that I hadn't noticed before.

"Is that so?" I asked her. "I can tell you're happy about it, so that must mean you said yes."

Juanita's face lit up with a big smile. "Yeah. I really like Rudy a lot, and I've never gone steady before."

"What does going steady mean these days?" I asked her.

"Well, I guess we're like boyfriend, girlfriend, and we're not supposed to date anyone else."

"I see. When did Rudy ask you to go steady?" I

knew that Juanita's father didn't allow her to date yet.

"A few weeks ago I went with Maya to the mall and we met Tyrone, that's Maya's boyfriend, and Rudy. Then we all walked over to the park across from the mall."

Juanita became silent for a minute. She had a serious look on her face. "I hate sneaking around. I was scared the whole time that my brother Carlos or someone would see me at the park with Rudy and then I'd really get in trouble."

"Do you think it's worth sneaking around if it makes you feel so uncomfortable?" I asked her. What a stupid question. Even I knew the answer to that.

"I don't know, Ms. Martínez. I just wish my dad wasn't so strict. He won't even let me go to school dances. He says I'm too young."

My heart went out to Juanita. My parents had treated me the same way, telling me they wouldn't let me date until I was eighteen. They had forced me into lying and sneaking around. I had always felt guilty about it, just like Juanita was feeling now.

"Do you think that maybe your mom can help you convince your dad that it's okay to go out sometimes, like to supervised dances?" I asked.

"No way, Ms. Martínez. My dad's the boss. Even my 'Amá won't change his mind."

"Is there anyone else in the family he might listen to?"

"Not really. But I keep thinking that maybe when I'm sixteen he'll see that I'm more grown-up and he'll let me go out more."

"That's not for a whole year. What will you do

meantime, Juanita?"

"I don't know, Ms. Martínez. I really want to keep seeing Rudy. He's so nice. But I guess I have to be careful so I don't get caught with him. 'Apá would kill me."

"It sounds like it's getting serious between you and Rudy?"

Juanita blushed. "We made out, that's all."

"What does 'making out' mean?"

"Just kissing. Some girls let the guys pet them, I guess, but I'm not stupid. I plan on staying a virgin for a long time."

"Good for you, Juanita. I know that it's easy to get pressured into doing something you're not ready for. Are you able to talk about sex with your mom?"

Juanita frowned. "I can't, Ms. Martínez. That would really be embarrassing."

"Well, how about with Maya?"

"A little bit. Last year in our health classes we talked about it."

Juanita's face was turning red, and she kept avoided my eyes. I decided that it was time to change the subject. "Well, Juanita, maybe that's something we can continue talking about in our meetings this year. That is, if you want to."

"Yeah, okay," Juanita mumbled, pulling at her skirt.

"Now, I wanted to talk a little bit about going back to school. Sam is convinced that we have such a good case, the school board is going to make a decision real soon in your favor."

"I sure hope so. I can hardly wait to go back to school. I'll never let myself get involved in a fight again."

"That's great, Juanita. But I wanted to ask you how you will feel about being around Sheena again? What is going to happen when you see her at school?"

Juanita was silent for a moment before answering, "I don't hate Sheena. Even after everything that happened, I kinda feel sorry for her."

"Well, what will you do when you see her in the halls? Or what if you have a class with her?"

"I'm going to ignore her, I guess. And if she tries to start trouble, I'll go tell the teacher."

"That's a smart thing to do, Juanita, to control your anger just like you did that night at the dance club. It's better to walk away than to get involved in something that could get out of control. You also need to remember that the teachers are there to help you."

"Yeah, I know. I won't be so stupid anymore. If I have to, I'll go to my counselor."

"Good for you, Juanita. And I hope you'll always trust me and call me if you need help."

Juanita smiled. "Thanks, Ms. Martínez. I really like you. Someday I want to be just like you."

I laughed. "Oh, you poor thing! I'm just kidding. Thank you, Juanita. That's the nicest compliment anyone has ever given me. Now, young lady, it looks like we've run out of time. Do you need a ride home? It's really raining out there."

"Yeah, if it's okay with you."

"My pleasure. Let's get going before the weather gets any worse."

TWENTY-SIX
Ms. Martínez

The following day, I was just getting ready to leave my office when the phone started ringing. "Damn," I muttered to myself, reaching for the receiver. I detested those last-minute calls at the end of the day.

"Hello," I answered, sounding as rude as I could.

"Sandra, It's Sam. I have great news. We won. Dr. Larson called me today. The school board has decided to reinstate Juanita after spring break."

"Yes!" I screamed into the telephone. "Sam, that's wonderful! Have you told Juanita yet?"

"Yes. I just got off the phone with her. She's just as excited as you are."

I felt my eyes fill with tears, and for a brief moment, I couldn't speak. There was justice after all. I suddenly felt like I could continue to hope, to dream, to believe in myself.

"Sandra, are you still there?" asked Sam.

"Yes, Sam. I can't tell you how happy I'm feeling. And I don't even know how I can begin to thank you, Sam. You donated all your time. I know the Chávezes feel so grateful to you."

"We did it together, Sandra. I couldn't have

done it without your help. You're from that culture, and you gave me important insights. I'm just glad to know that there are professional people of color like you who haven't forgotten their community."

"Thank you, Sam. This has been quite an experience for me."

"Now, one last thing, Sandra. It's very important that you continue your sessions with Juanita for the rest of the year. The school board wanted reassurance that you would continue to counsel her."

We both laughed. "Yes, I know that game plan. Don't change the system, just rehabilitate them."

"Sandra, I have to go now, but I'll get in touch with you later."

"Thanks again, Sam," I said, hanging up the phone. I grabbed my briefcase and hurried out the door.

It was raining lightly when I stepped outside, but I didn't care. The only thing I could think about was Juanita. I climbed into my old Volkswagen and drove straight to her apartment.

When I knocked on the door, Celia opened the door and invited me inside. Juanita was talking on the telephone, but as soon as she saw me she hung up and ran to my side. I held out my arms and gave her a giant hug.

"Ms. Martínez, I'm so happy. Thank you for everything. I just told Maya. She's excited, too."

"You don't know how excited I am! Have you told your parents?"

"Not yet. They're still working. They'll get home about seven. I can hardly wait to tell them the news."

"I'm so happy for you, Juanita. It's been a long battle, but we did it."

"Would you like to sit down, Ms. Martínez? How about some coffee?" Juanita asked, suddenly remembering her manners.

"No, thank you, Juanita. I want to hurry home and tell Frank. He's going to be so excited for us. Now, did Sam tell you that we need to continue our counseling sessions?"

"Yeah. I'm glad 'cause I really like talking with you."

"Good I do, too. Now I better get going before my husband thinks he doesn't have a wife anymore."

Juanita gave me another hug. "Thanks, Ms. Martínez."

"You don't need to thank me, Juanita. Just invite me to your graduation."

Juanita's face lit up. "I sure will!"

I gave Juanita one last hug and hurried out the door.

✎   ✐   ✎

That evening, Frank insisted we celebrate. I put on the sexy black dress that Frank had given me for Christmas, and we went to our favorite Chinese restaurant.

Frank ordered champagne, and we spent the next half-hour toasting to Juanita's future, to Sam Turner, to the Roosevelt school board, and to our lives together.

"She couldn't have done it without you, Sandy," Frank said.

"That's not true. I hardly did anything. Sam did all the work."

"Come on, Sandy, you donated your time just

like Sam, on top of all that stress you have with your patients."

"I did it because I cared."

"I know, hon. That's why I love you so much. Because you care so much about people, and especially about those who need help the most, like Juanita's family."

Frank kissed me then, and I found myself needing him more than I ever had.

✎ ✑ ✎

Before going to bed that evening, I picked up the phone and dialed my parents' number.

"Hello."

"Hello, Mom. It's me, Sandy. I hope I didn't wake you."

"No, you didn't. I was just getting ready for bed."

"How's Dad?" I asked her.

"He's fine. He misses you."

"Well, I just called to tell you that Frank and I are coming up to spend Easter vacation with you."

I heard the joy in my mother's voice. "Oh, Sandy, that's wonderful. Your dad will be so glad. *M'ija*, I'm so glad you're coming, Frank, too."

"Me, too, Mom. I miss both of you. And Mom, there's something else I wanted to tell you."

"What, *m'ija*?"

"I love you, Mom."

There was a moment of silence. Then in a low voice, I heard my mother say, "I love you, too, Sandra."

I hung up the phone, feeling happier than I'd been in a very long time.

TWENTY-SEVEN
Juanita

I feel so restless. It seems like spring break is
never going to end. I keep counting the days until
school starts again. Carlos thinks I'm crazy to want
to go back. 'Amá and 'Apá are both so happy that I
am going back to Roosevelt. 'Apá already told his
friends that when I graduate, he's having a big
party. 'Amá was so happy when I told them the
news that she cooked a special dinner for Ms.
Martínez and her husband. 'Amá made her deli-
cious *sopes,* stuffed tortillas, and we all laughed
'cause Frank, that's what Ms. Martínez calls him,
ate ten of them. He broke the record for eating
'Amá's *sopes!* 'Amá made some hot chile, too, and
Frank kept eating it until his face was red and
sweaty. Ms. Martínez kept laughing at him. I really
like Ms. Martínez. Someday I want to be just like
her. Well, almost like her. I don't want to be a
shrink, but I want to be smart and pretty like her.

✎   ✐   ✎

On Easter Sunday, 'Amá, Celia, me, and the little ones went to church. 'Amá says that we must
give thanks to the *Virgen de Guadalupe* for bring-

ing us good luck. After church, 'Apá drove us to
Lake San Martin and we had our yearly Easter picnic. Celia and I hid Easter eggs for the little ones.
Carlos thought he was too grown up to help us, so
he just watched. Afterwards, we all stuffed ourselves with Easter candy.

Later that night, I was so excited that I
couldn't sleep. I wondered if everyone at school
would stare at me. I wondered how I'd feel when I
saw Sheena. I was so nervous that I woke up real
early the next morning.

While I was in the shower, I remembered what
Ms. Martínez told me one time. "Be yourself,
Juanita, and everything will be all right." I hurried
and got dressed. Then I woke Celia. As Carlos goes
into the bathroom, he teases me that I'm going to
be late.

Downstairs, the three little ones are watching
cartoons and 'Amá is in the kitchen. She insists
that I eat an egg. I hate eggs, but I feel so happy
that I agree.

At exactly seven-thirty, I head for the street
corner to meet my friends. Tyrone, Tommy, and
Rina are already standing there waiting for me.

"You're sure looking hot," Tyrone tells me.

Tommy whistles at me and Rina punches him.
"Shut up," I tell Tommy jokingly. I'm so excited to
be with my friends again that I don't even mind
hearing them talk about how much they hate math
or old Mrs. Plumb.

When I get to my locker, Maya is waiting for
me. She hugs me and starts screaming, "*¡Órale!
¡Órale!*" I laugh so hard at her that my stomach
hurts. The bell rings and I hurry to my English
class. As I walk in, Mrs. Stevens says, "Welcome

back, Juanita." I thank her and sit down in the empty seat behind Carla. Mrs. Stevens starts talking about adverbial clauses. Carla leans forward and whispers to me, "This is so boring." I can't help but smile, feeling glad that I'm here and not somewhere else.

The morning goes by quickly. I don't feel as nervous by the time I get to my fourth period class. At first everyone in my Spanish class stares at me, but after a little while they forget about me and start talking about what they did during spring break. Then Mrs. Plumb yells, "*¡Silencio!*" She looks straight at me and says, "*Bienvenida, chica.*" I hear Maya giggling at Mrs. Plumb's spanish pronunciation. I say "*muchas gracias, Señora* Plumb," and whisper, "Shut up" to Maya, who is sitting behind me.

After our Spanish class, Maya and I race to our lockers to drop off our books. We grab our lunch bags and head out to our old meeting place. We are turning the corner when I see Sheena walking toward me with a friend. Before I have time to decide how to act, Sheena nods at me and walks past me. I feel a sudden relief. Ms. Martínez was right. It's not good to be angry. I don't hate Sheena. Maybe someday we can be friends again.

When we get to our old meeting place, everyone is waiting for us. Ankiza makes room for me to sit next to her and Rina.

"Hey, Johnny, we missed you," Ankiza says. "Thanks," I tell her, unwrapping my bologna sandwich. Then Tommy reaches over and grabs my Ding-Dong out of my lunch bag.

"Welcome back, Juanita," he teases me. "I missed you too."

Rina looks at him and says, "*¡Cochino!*"

We all start laughing. Rudy looks over at me and asks me how it feels to be back. Before I can answer him, Rina says, "How do you think, *pendejo*?"

"Shut up, Rina," Maya yells.

"Did you check out Mrs. Plumb's see-through blouse this morning?" Rina asks us. "And she doesn't even have boobs!"

"God, you're so gross, Rina," says Tyrone.

We are all laughing again. It feels so good to be back in school again, to be back with my friends, even if they are gross!

Glossary

Adiós—goodbye
'Amá—mother
'Apá—father

baboso—idiot; dummy; saliva-face
barrio—an Hispanic neighborhood
¡Bienvenida, chica!—Welcome, young lady!
Buenas tardes.—Good afternoon.

chaparra—shortly
Chicano (a)—a person of Mexican descent living
  in the U.S. who has a political consciousness
  related to Chicano issues and those of other ethnic minorities
cholo (a)—modern day Mexican/Chicano youth
  who dresses distinctively and rebels against
  mainstream culture; a modern day "Pachuco (a)"
cochino (a)—a pig; a slob
¿Cómo está, Señora Chávez?—How are you,
  Mrs. Chávez?
compadre (s)—the godfather of someone's child

Está bien.—That's fine.
Están locas.—You're all crazy.

gabacho—Anglo-American; gringo
gracias—thank you
gringo—Anglo-American
güero—a light skinned or fair-haired person; a light-complected Chicano

hija—daughter
¡Híjole!—Wow! My goodness! Oh my gosh!
hola—hello

m'ija—the contraction of "my daughter"
Muchas gracias.—Thank you very much.

Norteñas—Tex-Mex music; a type of music typical of states bordering the United States

Ojos de Dios—a religious Christmas tree ornament that evolved in indigenous cultures that symbolizes the "eye of the creator"
¡Órale!—Hey!; Okay!; Right on! All right!

pan dulce—Mexican sweet bread
pipí—pee pee
pobrecita—you poor thing
posadas (Las)—a Mexican celebration over a period of days in which the birth of Jesus is reenacted.

¡Qué vergüenza!—How embarrassing! How humiliating!

Raza—Race; lineage; family; La Raza includes all Latinos regardless of nationality; literally, the race of people
Rosa Salvaje—a popular Mexican soap opera, starring Verónica Castro

Sábado gigante—a popular Saturday night variety show on Spanish television hosted by Don Francisco
silencio—silence
sopes—a deep fried corn tortilla filled or topped with beans, rice, etc.

tamal (es)—tamale, tamales
tía—aunt

Virgen de Guadalupe—Mexico's most honored patron saint; the indigenous, brown-skinned Virgin Mary

Gloria Velásquez created the Roosevelt High School Series "so that young adults of different ethnic backgrounds would find themselves visible instead of invisible. When I was growing up, there weren't any books with characters with whom I could relate, characters that looked or talked like Maya, Juanita, or Ankiza. The Roosevelt High School Series [RHS] is my way of promoting cultural diversity as well as providing a forum for young people to discuss serious issues that impact their lives. I often will refer to the RHS Series as my 'Rainbow Series' since I modeled it after Jesse Jackson's concept of the rainbow coalition."

Velásquez has received numerous honors for her writings and achievements, such as being featured for Hispanic Heritage Month on KTLA, Channel 5, Los Angeles, an inclusion in *Who's Who Among Hispanic Americans, Something About the Author* and *Contemporary Authors*. In 1989, Velásquez became the first Chicana to be inducted into the University of Northern Colorado's Hall of Fame. The 2003 anthology, *Latina and Latino Voices in Literature for Teenagers and Children*, devotes a chapter to Velásquez's life and development as a writer. Velásquez is also featured in the 2006 PBS Documentary, *La Raza de Colorado*. In 2004, Velásquez was featured in "100 History Making Ethnic Women" by Sherry Park (Linworth Publishing). Stanford University recently honored her with "The Gloria Velásquez Papers," archiving her life as a writer and humanitarian.